DESIRE, DECEPTION AND REVENGE

RITA CLARK JOHNSON

This novel is a work of fiction. Names, characters, places and incidents are a product of the author's imagination or are used fictionally. Any resemblance to actual events, locales or persons, living or dead, is entirely coincidental.

Library of Congress Cataloging – in – Publication Data

Johnson, Rita C.

Desire, Deception and Revenge

Desire, Deception and Revenge

For those who do not have a voice, and

For those who do, but cannot speak

Acknowledgments

This novel has been a labor of love over several lifetimes, hills and valleys. I have my dear friend Karen Jones Curry to thank for encouraging me to continue this labor of love, and who read my first incomplete draft. My next heartfelt thanks is to another dear but equally treasured friend, Mary Davis Edelin, who read my manuscript almost overnight. Mary's suggestion to add a twist was truly inspirational and added to an interesting ending. At times I felt I couldn't keep up with her. I would be remiss if I didn't also mention Brian Davis who graciously offered me countless hours of support and his know how in this endeavor. My final nod goes to Kyle S. Johnson, my son, and RheQuan Robinson, whom I give artistic credit too.

Table of Contents

Characters

1. Angelique Dupre Sterling – "Angel"

2. Michelle Dupre – Angelique's Mother

3. Jack Montenero – Michelle's friend, later husband

4. Paul Monroe – Angel's significant love from teen years

5. Josh Sterling – Angel's Ex, Kimmie's dad

6. Kimberly "Kimmie" Sterling – Angel's daughter

7. Vivian Summervale – "Viv" Angel's best friend

8. Jamal Leonard – Vivian's love interest

9. Edward Morgan – "Eddy" – NY editor

10. Amelia Ross – Paul's hospital nurse

11. Raphael Medici – Paul's godfather, shrewd businessman

12. Serita Rodriguez Monroe – Paul's mom, exotic, fragile

13. Kyle Monroe – Paul's dad

14. Damien Dupre – Angelique's "Benefactor"

15. Jamari Dupre – Angel's dad

16. Dr. Judith Barnes – Paul's doctor, Chief of Neurosurgery

17. Monique Dubois – Paul's former girlfriend

18. Joe – Manager of ski chalet

19. Capt. Maxwell F. Franklin – "Fierce Franklin," friend of Angel

20. Ted – Vivian's assistant with fundraising

21. Lt. Arnold – assigned to kidnapping case

22. Officer Wayne – police investigator

23. Anjare, Ray, Selena, Andre, Michael – minor introductory characters

24. Dr. Helen and Atty. Gerald Morgan – Edward's parents

Bound location – Society Island in the South Pacific

Prologue

Silently she walked through the house one last time, memorizing each room and imprinting them forever to memory. The night before she had swept and re-swept each room, remembering the once gleaming hardwood floors of her childhood. She had swept relentlessly, slipping back to a time when joy and laughter were her constant companions. That was before Paul, before the abduction. Desperately she tried to cling to the present memories of her past. But they belonged to a happier era.

This was the second home Angelique Dupre had loved and cherished and was compelled to abandon. The third time in her short-lived years she would have to begin again with no direction. Staring at her reflection in the mirror of the downstairs bath Angelique was shocked by what she saw. Her face still possessed a youthful look far younger than her twenty - nine years, and the strain of her ordeals. There were no lines yet about her eyes. Her skin, still taut, held the glow of youth, and her luscious shoulder length auburn hair held no trace of gray. But those eyes!

"The eyes are the mirror of the soul, and you have the most innocent yet mysterious eyes I've ever seen," murmured Paul, that cold December day when they first met. Angelique smiled shyly up at him in response. Her almond shaped orbs, hazel with a hint of green, made Angelique appear soft and seductive one moment, cold and calculating the next. That was thirteen years ago. Now these same eyes only mirrored the raw horror she had been forced to live.

Shaking her head deliberately to chase those cobweb memories away, Angel, as her close friends affectionately called her, still gazed at her reflection staring back at her. Her skin was naturally bronzed, inherited from her Polynesian mother and French Moroccan father. A union that held just long enough to produce her. Angel had not known her father well. Jamari had been too busy with his flourishing import export business to bother with a moody yet spirited child. Her mother, Michelle, on the other hand, doted on Angelique, trying to give the love of two parents. But that was before the monstrous tragedy that was to alter Angelique's life a second time.

Chapter One

In The Beginning

Michelle

The Boeing 747 carrying Angelique Dupre had touched down at National Airport in Washington, D.C. It was the dead of winter. This day marked the coldest in recorded history for the area, and the start of Angelique's life in the United States. Each breath the tiny child expelled attempted to freeze in midair. Snow covered everything in sight for miles around. The wind whipped unmercifully at her frail body, heaping mounds of snow at eerie angles, creating drifts as much as four feet high. A limousine provided by Jamari, Michelle's estranged husband, promptly arrived and the statuesque woman with her toddler was quickly whisked away. Home became a small apartment in Georgetown, a quaint but impressive area in Washington, D.C. known for its beautiful architecture and history. This was to be a temporary haven for the pair until more suitable quarters could be found.

Until now Angel's ears had been accustomed to the lilting intonation of her mother's French and Berber Tamazight languages. But this new language was babble to her ears. Before long, however, Angel learned English and spoke it fluently. Michelle quickly established herself and became the owner of one of Georgetown's most lucrative and chic boutiques, The Chez Paris, filled with original creations from all over Europe.

Along with Michelle's continuing success came several moves. The last was to McLean, Virginia, a remote suburb of metropolitan Washington, D.C. McLean is home to senators, congressmen and many influential businessmen whose wives insisted on being dressed by the fabulous Michelle. Very often she was invited to attend numerous functions given by the women she dressed. Many times she would simply make an appearance for the sake of her business. But one invitation came that she immediately accepted, a poolside party at the home of a very good friend.

"This party will allow me to relax and unwind," mused Michelle.

No one would be trying to impress her with who he or she was or whom he or she was married to. The timing was perfect! There was no upcoming showing and Michelle had just returned from a buying trip abroad. She was totally free. Michelle knew everyone who attended the party with the exception of one man who had arrived late and had immediately become ensconced with several of the businessmen who gravitated toward one another.

"My God, what a beauty!" Jack exclaimed to himself at the sight of Michelle. He had been too busy earlier closing a deal to circulate at the party he attended merely for the advantageous gathering.

Jack was immediately entranced by Michelle in her seductive white one-piece bathing suit, cut high to reveal her long, slender shapely legs. Her hair was piled high in a carefree fashion with tendrils framing her exquisite face and accentuating her long slender neck. Their meeting was brief, but an electric current seemed to pass between them. Jack was powerful yet appeared gentle and kind. This was something Michelle had never sensed in other men of power. Powerful men were usually ruthless, cold and calculating in their dealings, and carried this same attitude with them in their relationships.

Somehow without even realizing it, Michelle had accepted a dinner invitation with a man she had met and talked with for no more than ten minutes. He was gone now. He had left soon after their conversation ended. But all the while his eyes had mesmerized her as she had listened to his deep resonant voice. As he strode off, she watched the sinewy muscles ripple in his back beneath his short-sleeved shirt. Now that the elusive stranger was gone their brief interlude didn't seem real.

Jack

Jack Montenero. A swarthy, rather handsome man of olive complexion and black brooding eyes, deep set in his chiseled face. His hair is thick and black with one unruly curl which falls seductively yet boyishly across his forehead. Spawned from Bolivian parents, this enigmatic man walks with an air of arrogance and supreme confidence. Although Jack is not very tall like the men Michelle is usually attracted to, she cannot help but be drawn to this extremely intriguing man. Jack is built compact yet muscular, with broad shoulders that taper to a slim waist with no hint of a paunch. He is in as excellent shape as is his portfolio. His wealth, from an undetermined source, seems endless, as Jack is known to travel the continents for business and much pleasure in his personal jet, complete with bodyguards.

Promptly at 7:00 Jack appeared on Michelle's doorstep. He had called at 5:00 that evening as promised and had earlier sent a small bouquet of black orchids. Michelle was an exquisite creature he meant to have, and he was used to getting what he wanted. The other women in his life had been beautiful, but none possessed the drive and independence he sensed in Michelle. She had to be a strong woman to have accomplished what she had in the relatively short time she had been in this country.

Jack's assistant did a confidential background check on Michelle, customary because of Jack's position. It revealed little that Jack did not already know. Here was a young woman of humble origins who, through sheer wit and determination, had become highly successful in her chosen career. Michelle had married young and became a single parent seemingly overnight. Her ability to single-mindedly overcome the many obstacles in her path destined Michelle to come out on top. Jack admired her for her accomplishments, but said nothing of this to her. Most people, he knew, would not respond kindly to having their lives scrutinized.

Dinner was uneventful. Or more truthfully, it was as if two old friends were being reacquainted after some time apart. There was none of the awkwardness that usually accompanies a first date. The waterfront restaurant, Fiola Mare, located in Washington, D.C., was tastefully elegant. Jack chose a table in a corner near an expansive window so they could gaze at the stars just peeping into view. They dined by candlelight, each exploring the other's personality. Jack told whimsical anecdotes that made Michelle laugh and feel like she was sixteen again. Michelle told Jack of her schooling in a convent as a young girl and of the many pranks she had pulled, all the while maintaining an angelic face to the nuns.

"I'm sure their prayers went into overtime for my soul many nights," she said with a languid smile. "I'm very glad you asked me to dinner tonight," Michelle stated.

"I'm even happier you accepted, replied Jack."

And as if an afterthought Jack added, "I thought for a moment you would refuse, and I would have to devise some devilish scheme to kidnap you for a few hours." A fleeting look of shock crossed her face momentarily until Michelle realized she had been subjected to Jack's deadpan humor, as she caught the twinkle in his eye.

"Tell me a secret," she whispered into his ear as they began to leave the restaurant, "and make it a good one."

Abruptly Jack stopped, turned and hesitated just long enough to decide. A small furrow deepened in his brow.

"I'm in love with you, and I've never, ever been in love before."

With that said Jack reached for Michelle's hand and gently led her, dumbfounded, into the cool night air. From that moment on she was his and he was hers. There was no mistaking the sincerity in his voice or the caring in his eyes.

Jack and Michelle. They were a well-matched pair. Each had their own lives and concerns, but each made time for the other. The circle comfortably included Angelique who now frequently traveled with the couple to the many exotic places that had become ordinary to Jack. Now the many places took on an air of excitement and intrigue. It was as if Jack was discovering a gem for the very first time, which had all the while been in the palm of his hand. Michelle was good for him and he thankfully had the sense to realize it.

Good was not the word to describe the effect Jack had on Michelle and Angelique. He was right for the both of them. There was a completeness in all their lives. A void created from loneliness and longing had been fulfilled. "Someday," Michelle would promise, when the subject of marriage would inevitably come up. "I'm not sure I'm ready yet," was her constant reply. Michelle had divorced Jamari years ago now, but the sting of that failure remained.

Deep down Michelle was afraid their relationship would turn sour with marriage, as Michelle's marriage to Jamari had. Michelle and Jamari should never have been. But what happened was a lifetime ago. Michelle often fleetingly thought of her first love, Damien, but as her dream of being with him had vanished, so had her true love. Jack and Michelle were together now. They wanted to be together, not because of a *silly piece of paper*, but because they cared deeply for one another. Michelle could not undo the hurt and confusion of her past. Her long, lost love was forever lost to her. Her marriage had failed. She had to move on, and she had done so with Jack.

"You snore when you're asleep," Michelle teased, "and in my sleep I might think a burglar is in the house and shoot you." With a sly grin she added, "No, we'd better keep living apart," she murmured to Jack's repeated suggestions she move into his mansion. "Besides, this way I can keep you guessing!" Jack resided on 15 acres of scarce waterfront property in an area between Old Town Alexandria and George Washington's Mount Vernon in Virginia, replete with vast pastoral treelined areas sloping to the Potomac River. His home was magnificent with the French-provincial style reminiscent of grand estates that were built centuries before. It included an olympic pool, a heliport, a fully stocked pond, a private dock and beach with views along the Potomac River toward a wooded Maryland Shore.

Jack muttered an obscenity under his breath and playfully swatted Michelle's behind with a large pillow. This last antic was one of their favorite ways of breaking the tension. There was nothing better than an old-fashioned pillow fight, with Angelique siding with first one then the other, depending on who was losing miserably at the time. In the morning the trio was taking off for a skiing trip to Jack's chalet in Montana. He had become a member of the Yellowstone Club in the Rockies. This limited-membership club with an initial fee of $400,000.00 and an annual fee of $41,500.00 afforded Jack the privacy he required. He may occasionally bump into notables such as Bill Gates or Justin Timberlake on a ski lift. Otherwise, this exclusive club gave Jack the solitude he sought after whirlwind business negotiations.

Michelle wondered how long Angel would want to accompany her and Jack on these family trips. At seventeen Angel was gorgeous. She was slim with small breasts, a tiny waist and provocative hips that swayed to and fro with many promises when she walked. One couldn't help but stare at her heart shaped face, complete with doe-like almond shaped eyes fringed with lush, full, curly lashes, a slightly snub nose and sensuous full lips that invited a kiss. But Angelique was oblivious to all this. She still possessed a childlike spirit and naiveté. Like most teenagers, Angel was insecure about her appearance. She had dated but had not had a serious love…yet.

Chapter Two

A Taste of Love

Angelique

It was during this trip that Angelique first tasted the rush and thrill of the new sensuality surging through her body. Jack, Michelle and Angel had decided to suit up immediately for the slopes upon their arrival at the chalet. Jack was the first to smoothly descend the difficult course. Michelle, athletically toned and strikingly beautiful, had no difficulty on the course either. Angel was an accomplished skier also, but something happened on this run. Suddenly a high-pitched scream splintered the still air, unheard by Jack or Michelle who were too far away. Appearing as if from nowhere, a dark-haired stranger was immediately at her side. He did not immediately attempt to move her but made sure she was okay before helping her to her feet.

"I'm fine," Angel insisted. "I just had the wind knocked out of me.

But as her rescuer helped her to her feet Angel stumbled into him, sending his blood coursing through his body at a fevered pitch. Even in snow gear, she was the most beautiful creature he had ever seen. Regretfully, he stared into her eyes longer than was comfortable for either of them.

Unknown to Jack or Michelle, Paul had followed at a discrete distance after spotting Angelique arriving at the chalet. It had not been sheer luck he had been nearby to help her, but coincidental that Angel fell in a spot so close to where this stranger stood. After awkward introductions, Paul and Angelique slowly descended the slope together. He had been trying to think of a way to meet this childlike woman from the moment he first spotted her, when fate all but handed her to him.

"Who are you and what are you doing here?" bellowed Jack. From his scowl and the frown reflected on Michelle's face, Paul knew he was an unwanted intruder.

"The name is Paul, Paul Monroe. I'm working here on the mountain. I heard a scream. That's when I found this young lady face down in the snow."

Angel blushed at the mention of the accident. "I just lost my balance somehow and fell; I'm okay."

"I'm glad you're okay," Paul said, "but I still don't know your name."

"Sorry, my name is Angelique, Angel to my friends, and this is my mother, Michelle Dupre and our friend Jack Montenero. I apologize for not thanking you sooner for helping me back on the slope."

"Don't thank me; I'm just glad I was there to help you," said Paul.

"I'm grateful to you for helping my daughter too," chimed Michelle. "You must forgive our rude behavior. It's just that no one else is to be visiting on the mountain at this time."

"That's true," Paul said, "but I was hired on to work in the common lodge during my semester break from school."

Without a further exchange the four entered the rustic ski lodge just at the bottom of the slope, each with a different feeling about the events that had just taken place. Jack had gone to great lengths and expense exclusively renting this week to ensure their seclusion and safety. Paul's name had not appeared in the list of employees his assistant had given him for clearance. How had this person managed to get through the tight network of security and intelligence Jack had maintained for so long? That question would burn in Jack's mind for many years to come.

The remainder of the trip proved uneventful. Jack's security turned up insignificant information on the mysterious Paul Monroe. He was twenty, a third-year college student attending Amherst College, a small school in Amherst, MA offering an open curriculum and committed to meeting 100% of demonstrated student need for all accepted students. It was one of the only three schools to reach the number one ranking among *U.S. News'* best small colleges. Paul attended the school on an academic scholarship but had to work to supplement the funding he received.

Paul

Angel found Paul exciting and daring with his stories of his childhood travels to many foreign countries as an Army brat. Even Michelle relaxed her usually close guard with the seemingly harmless young man and was not so disturbed by Paul's sudden appearance now. Jack remained skeptical, but Michelle now welcomed Paul for the company he provided her daughter. Angel, who kept to herself most of the time, had not brought a friend along on this trip and needed the companionship of someone closer to her own age. But Michelle did not know of the moonlight kisses and passionate embraces Paul and Angelique shared.

To Angel it seemed as if she had known Paul all of her life. For the first time, she opened up and dropped her defensive shyness. Paul made talking and being together so easy. All the high school boys she knew had made her feel self-conscious. They were acutely aware of her beauty and fumbled for words much of the time, in awe of her. Paul, on the other hand, made her feel comfortable. He did not treat her as a porcelain doll. Their camaraderie was so natural. On the last night of the holiday they met in their usual place, an old gnarled fir tree just in back of the lodge. Here they would meet to go snowmobiling or just walk and talk hand in hand. But this meeting was different. There was a growing urgency in Paul's eyes.

"Angel, there's so much I want to say to you, but I don't know where to begin." Taking a deep breath Paul continued, "I didn't mean to let things get out of control this way, but sometimes we can't stop things once they've been put in motion." Looking distraught, he continued, "I haven't been totally honest with you or myself...until now."

Struggling with inner turmoil, Paul remained quiet for a time. When he spoke again his voice was filled with longing and dread.

"One day you'll understand, and I hope you will forgive me."

Angelique stood completely still, trying to understand the puzzling things Paul was saying. What had been put in motion? What hadn't he been honest about?

"I want you to remember me when I'm gone."

As the words came out, he slipped his arm around Angel and turned her around to face him. Their eyes met. She felt his warm sweet breath on her cheek and in a moment, she was in Paul's arms. His mouth came down on hers gently at first, then more forcefully as his passion grew. They were both oblivious to the chill in the air as Angel clung to him for what seemed an eternity.

"The eyes are the mirror of the soul," murmured Paul, "and you have the most innocent yet mysterious eyes I've ever seen." Angelique smiled shyly up at him in response. Her almond shaped orbs, hazel with a hint of green, made Angelique appear soft and seductive one moment, cold and calculating the next. Suddenly she broke free of his embrace. His hands had begun to softly caress her neck and shoulders.

"Stop," Angel moaned in a husky voice, trembling from head to foot as the heat of passion swept over her. "We should go in now."

"Please stay," he murmured softly in her ear, as he released his grip on her. Holding up his hands in protest he flashed a playful smile, "Boy Scout's honor, we'll just walk and be together. It will be a long time before I see you again."

The sun had long since gone down, leaving a clear blue sky beginning to darken and glisten with a sprinkling of stars. Angel and Paul walked hand in hand in silence. Her heart was pounding in her chest as she tried to make sense of the new feelings surging through her young body. She could still feel each searing caress from Paul's fingertips burning into her flesh. Never before had she been so strongly aroused or divided. She yearned to give herself to Paul, but a part of her was not ready.

Paul was an extremely sensuous man in every sense of the word. His eyes were like liquid pools of velvet one would gladly drown in. Of Italian, Eritrean and Latin descent, Paul was tall, powerfully built with broad shoulders and possessed a ruddy complexion. By the play of downy hair on his arms Angelique fought the desire to play in the strands of curly black silk she imagined covering his chest. Suddenly she became aware of Paul's voice. She had heard not a word he had been saying until then. She had been dueling with her emotions, while studying the sensuous curve of his lips, now parted to reveal a row of perfectly white teeth.

Chapter Three

Betrayal

Paul had been so very sweet, and so convincing. Angelique trusted him completely, and much too soon. He had magically appeared in her life on the ski slope that ominous day of her accident. Why had she fallen? Had something been arranged to cause the seemingly minor incident that would bring the two of them together? Looking back, Angelique could only speculate on the events that led to her almost year long ordeal that was to plague her with nightmares for years to come.

~

The vacation had come to an end. This was the last day Angel would see Paul until his next semester break, several months away. The air was crisp and the morning clear, with the sun just peeking through the last mists of dawn. It was 5:30 and Angel wanted to get on the slopes before the other skiers who were due to arrive soon. After eating a light breakfast of muffins and hot tea she stepped from the coziness of the lodge into the chilly morning air to meet Paul at their usual rendezvous. He was already there when she arrived, and she was glad of his promptness.

In the two weeks she had gotten to know Paul she had begun to fall deeply in love with him. One swift glance at him told her something was troubling him. Paul looked as though something was on his mind this morning. Wanting the day to be upbeat, Angel shoved the questions from her mind. She wanted to simply enjoy the precious little time they still had together, this last day before they had to part. Angel raced up to Paul with skis and poles over her shoulder, dropped the whole bundle at his feet and gave him a bear hug and deep kiss. Sometimes she took him off guard with her lavish show of affection.

Paul was beginning to care deeply for Angel, and more than once dreaded doing what he knew he must.

"I want to show you something, something you haven't seen before," Paul teased.

"What is it?" she demanded.

"Just follow me, quietly if you can," and with that Paul led Angel into the forest until they came to a clearing. "There is a mother deer and her fawn nesting here..." was all she heard. Breaking free of the grasp of his hand, Angel began to walk ahead of Paul, excited at the thought of seeing the doe in its nest. Paul was telling Angelique he was sorry.

"I hadn't planned for things to happen this way," Paul said.

"What is he saying...? What does this mean?" thought Angelique.

A steady silence followed. Angel turned ever so slightly when she heard no more from Paul. Suddenly without a warning a gloved hand with a cloying scent was clamped over her mouth and nostrils. Panic seized her. Instinctively she clutched at the wrist holding the cloth to her face, desperately trying to loosen its hold. "Who is this, and why is this happening to me?" she wondered. Her mother had jealous rivals, but none who would stoop to...what was happening, anyway? Her back was to the assailant and she was pinned to him by an extremely strong grip. She felt as though she was in a vise.

Angelique could feel his breath warm on her neck as she struggled to be free. He couldn't be much taller than her, perhaps 5'7" or 5'8." The lessons in self-defense came quickly to mind, but they were useless in this circumstance. All she succeeded in doing was to break some sort of bracelet her attacker wore on his wrist. At this her assailant cursed quietly, revealing a foreign accent. It was an unusual accent, yet vaguely familiar to Angelique.

The harder she struggled the more she inhaled the noxious odor. The raw terror could be seen in her eyes as she valiantly struggled against the powerful arms that held her. Fear gave Angel unimaginable strength, but she was no match for the chloroform. Slowly she slipped into unconsciousness. She lay quiet now, all the fight gone from her. She had lost the battle. All that was left was a single tear coursing down her cheek. In a moment Angelique Dupre was limp, being carried by the gloved hands.

Angelique

Vaguely Angel remembered struggling with limbs that seemed to grow too heavy to move. Where she had been taken and for what purpose eluded her. Days dragged into weeks, weeks into months. She saw no one. The drab room that held Angel prisoner contained a single bed, commode and sink in the corner. The only window had been boarded up, save a crack in the board near the bottom. A pad and pencil had been shoved through the tiny opening under her door, and books to read had been provided her. Somehow the room was not stuffy. It was large but bare. One lamp had been placed in the room as if an afterthought. There were several pairs of jeans, all somewhat large for her small frame, and tops that were equally too large. Occasionally she heard voices muffled coming from somewhere beyond her door. They were angry voices.

"We had a deal, and this was not part of it!" came the hushed angry words.

Angel was pressed tightly against the door trying in vain to recognize the raspy voice that floated up to her. The sound seemed as if it was coming from close by, perhaps down the hall or even a staircase.

"Listen, I do as I'm told; the same as you! You'd better get used to it if you want to stay alive and keep your lover boy looks intact!! Your problem is you want the girl for yourself. That's not gonna happen and you know it."

"Yeah, yeah! I know all that. But if her old man ever wises up to who's behind his little darling's disappearance, we won't be alive two minutes to talk about it."

"Just keep your shirt on. Nobody's gonna find out anything if you just keep your trap shut."

"Shut up anyway! This place gives me the creeps."

Instantly all was quiet. Too quiet! The lights went off in her room as if the wires were suddenly cut. The silence was worse than the menacing sounds of her captors. Suddenly with no warning, the bolt on the door slid free. In one swift movement three tall, heavyset figures loomed in front of Angel. The blinding light from the huge lantern trained on her face made it impossible to see their faces. In another moment her hands and feet were bound and a hood that allowed no light was placed over her head. A quick, sharp pain jabbed Angel's arm. In seconds her entire body went limp. As if in slow motion, she felt herself falling, only to be caught by rough hands. Oblivion followed.

Chapter Four

Back in Time

Sunlight was streaming through the open window as Angelique stared with unseeing eyes at the passage she had just written for her new novel. The quiet hum of the early morning sounds catapulted her back in time. No longer was she the acclaimed novelist whose last five publications had been number one on the best seller's list. Gone for now was the poised woman who had overcome the harsh reality of living through a terrifying kidnapping. Angelique had been transported back in time. She was momentarily re-living the nightmare she had met at the hands of her captors so many years ago.

The bright chirping of the early morning birds had swept Angelique back to the Society Islands in the South Pacific that had been her jail. As the morning breeze swept over her face and arms, Angelique had again become the seventeen-year old girl whose world had been turned upside down over night. She had been violently snatched from her mother, Michelle, and had endured the separation for nearly a year.

The lush island jungle could have been a lovers' secluded paradise. For Angelique it was hell on earth. Here she celebrated her eighteenth birthday. It was here too that she had been psychologically tortured. Although Angel had managed to heal from her ordeal, she was never completely the same.

"Move it!" cried the southern drawl that made her flesh crawl. "Don't take all day with my food!"

Angel detested this horribly, inhuman person who was her daytime overseer. This gravelly, cruel voice was the main voice she heard the whole time she was held captive. Not only did she have to fight off his advances when she was made to serve him, but she had to endure his fiendish attempts to bed her at night as well. This masked fiend was always stopped in his attempts by a guard. It was obvious that whoever masterminded this scheme had not intended for Angel to be physically abused. She had been treated fairly well and had been isolated from the other young women who were held captive as well.

During the day Angelique was made to work in the kitchen of the large jungle plantation, but could never relax because of the gun-toting, machete waving guards posted outside all entrances to the kitchen. Each man was frighteningly dangerous. Each was powerfully built, with bulging biceps, broad shoulders and hands that could and would kill. These guards too wore masks to conceal their identities, and never spoke. The evil mastermind had taken great pains to ensure everyone's anonymity.

The two other girls who worked with Angelique spoke neither French nor English. All communication was by gesture. Angel felt more alone now than she had before she had been drugged and brought to this remote location. The island brought back vague memories reminiscent of her childhood home before coming to the states. But Angel had been too young when she left to realize she was on a neighboring island to her first home, Tahiti.

How could Angelique ever forget that awful time on the island? Here was where she truly grew up. Avoiding the advances and lewd suggestions she received all day from her daytime overseer whenever she left the safety of the kitchen was a monumental task. The nights were even worse. Angelique never saw the face of her *benefactor*, but she knew it was he who protected her. In a strange way she both hated and loved him. It was always pitch black in his chambers when she was brought to him. She could never see his face no matter how hard she tried. As an added protection against discovery he wore a smooth, dark mask, which completely covered his face.

"Tell me about yourself," was how their first encounter began. Angelique sat mute before her *benefactor*, refusing to speak. He spoke again in an accent strangely familiar to Angel.

"I will ask you one last time, and this time you will answer or there will be consequences."

With this said, the hooded, powerfully built man, with a soft, deep, resonant voice reclined on a chaise with an air of omnipotence. Angelique stammered out her reply as fear gripped her heart.

"There's not much to tell."

"Begin at the beginning," he growled out.

"My...my name is Angelique and..."

No sooner had she uttered her name, the hooded man suddenly sat straight up and peered at her closely. Angelique shrank from his gaze as his eyes bore into her.

"Why are you lying?" he demanded. "The truth, tell me the truth!"

Quite shaken by the fierceness in his voice, Angelique stammered out, "I'm Angelique Dupre." Tears pooled in her eyes and splashed like a river onto her hands, carefully clasped in her lap. She sat not two feet away, shrouded in the darkness of the chamber, lit by a single candle. The mystery man swore under his breath in that same foreign language, somewhat familiar to her, and bolted from the room through a curtained doorway to her right. Momentarily Angel sighed in relief. She didn't know or care why this man had acted so strangely. She hoped with all her might that he would release her. All hope vanished when the hooded man quickly appeared with some sort of garment in his massive hands.

The hooded man, unlike the other men she had seen on the island, was very tall. Since he wore a hood Angelique couldn't make out any facial features. "Put this on," he commanded, as he extended the garment to Angelique. She caught sight of the rippling muscles in his powerful biceps from the glow of the lone candle in the room. At one glance Angelique knew his strength was formidable. A pall settled over Angelique as she stood with resignation and slowly accepted the article from this strangely terrifying man.

Right before the hooded man's eyes Angelique changed from a timid gazelle to an assertive woman.

"No, I won't!" she replied defiantly.

Although Angelique was still frightened, her stubbornness and self-will took over. Unfolding himself from the chaise, the hooded man stood rigidly over Angelique. The anger emanating from him was almost palpable. It consumed and closed the small chasm that had separated the two. For some unknown reason he suddenly softened, ever so slightly. As he placed his hands on his hips and assumed a relaxed stance he spoke.

"You may call me Damien, mon petit," he murmured.

Did she hear him right? Why had he used a term of endearment? Angelique retreated a step. She had been ready, braced even, for a slap. Damien's subtle change startled her. Raising her face to peer intently into his eyes Angelique thought she saw a play of shifting emotions.

"What do you want from me?" she boldly asked.

Damien admired Angelique's strength of character and her refusal to cower to his demand. Gesturing toward the chaise he turned away from her as he spoke.

"Sit down...please. I won't hurt you. I can see you are young. Someone older and wiser would know to fear me."

Damien let his words sink in. Finally turning to face her he asked, "How old are you?"

"I'm seventeen," Angelique replied.

"The wrong one," she thought she heard Damien say. What did this mean? For the time being she kept quiet. She thought better of provoking this angry goliath.

As time passed Angelique began to look forward to her times with Damien. He was kind to her and never attempted to frighten her again after their initial exchange. Although he never physically abused her in any way, he made her submit to an odd ritual. Each time she was summoned to his chambers she was made to privately shed every article of western clothing, bathe, and adorn herself in one of the many shimmering, gossamer yet opaque gowns provided for her, replete with bangles, necklaces, earrings and head attire. At his insistence she also had to anoint herself in exotic perfumed oils and position herself at his feet on a pillow.

"Why must I wear these clothes?" Angelique demanded of his docile servant the next time she was brought to Damien's quarters. "I'm not putting that on!"

The only word the shy servant girl uttered was, "Must! Must!" There was so much trembling in the girl's voice and hands that Angelique thought better of defying the giant's request. It was clear to Angelique that the consequences of her not obeying this request would be dire to the girl, if not to herself also.

"Alright," she replied, extending her hand after noticing the fear in the young girl's eyes, "hand me the clothes." And with that the ritual began.

Angelique was grateful for the extremely dim lighting in the room because of her palpable fear. She imagined herself to look like one of the women in a harem of old. Little did Angelique know she fulfilled a twofold fantasy of the mighty Damien. In her he imagined the woman he loved and the child they would have had together. In all aspects Angelique was treated like a cherished porcelain doll while with Damien. He never touched her nor requested anything from her other than to listen to him. She was not to speak unless spoken to, though. Most of the time was spent with Damien attempting to brainwash Angelique against Jack Montenero and the world he stood for. Angelique wondered why Damien held such hostility toward Jack, and how he knew him. Caution and intuition held her tongue. It would be much wiser to listen and learn. Perhaps she would venture a question or two when Damien let his guard down, if he ever would.

In an odd way Angelique came to care for Damien. Although he frightened her at the start, he no longer seemed a threat to her. He was always mindful of her feelings and did not evoke the fear in her that he once had. Soon after their first encounter Angelique's overseer mistreated her by roughly twisting her arm. When word of the misdeed filtered back to Damien he dealt harshly with the thug, thus spreading his protective arm over Angel wherever she went on the isolated, sparsely inhabited island.

Angelique was never to learn that Damien her captor was in fact her long lost uncle. He had desperately loved Michelle, her mother, when they both were teenagers. He had asked Michelle to marry him long before Jamari, Michelle's father, came into Michelle's life. Angelique looked so much like her mother that at times Damien loved and hated Angelique in the same instance. But the thought that Angel could have been his daughter tore at his heart. Jack was merely the person who was able to win Michelle's heart and shower her with the love, affection and attention Damien so wished he could have given Michelle. Although he despised Jack for having Michelle, he could never forgive Jamari, his brother, for stealing from him the only woman he had ever loved.

In his private quarters with fists clenched Damien grapples with the torment of his soul. In a state of despair he shouts to the empty walls of his hideaway, "They must all pay for my misery!" From the depths of his lonely, aching heart Damien seeks the memory of Michelle for comfort and finds the reality of Angelique.

"I see your face everywhere," he whispers into the stillness, thinking only of Michelle. "Alone at night I see you here beside me, looking into my eyes with trust and desire. You believed in me, wanted me. All that is gone. I have been vanquished. But I will avenge those who stole my joy!" With pure malice on his face Damien continues, "I trusted Jamari, my brother, to look after you, my sweet Michelle, when I went off to fight in the war. But when I returned, I found Jamari had convinced you that I had died and would never return for you." Bowing his head in abject desolation, Damien covers his eyes with his massive hands as a river of tears flows freely down his anguished face. Jamari's deception is complete and evident in the presence of Angelique.

Chapter Five

The Abduction

Glancing at the illuminated dial of her alarm clock, Michelle noted it was only 6:30. The Morning sun should have been streaming through the lace curtains at the windows, but the sky was overcast. A light dusting of powdery snow was falling this last day of Angelique's winter break. Deciding to get an early start before their departure from the chalet, Michelle swung her shapely legs to the hardwood floor covered by handmade sheep skin rugs. Immediately she was struck by an intense wave of "evil." The emanating heat of the evil that engulfed her was so tangible she almost reached out to touch it. Shuddering from the strange experience, Michelle quickly looked around, as if expecting to find some ominous creature lurking nearby. Shrugging her shoulders to cast off the eerie feeling, Michelle hurriedly padded down the solemn, dark hallway to check on Angelique. Something she hadn't felt compelled to do in years.

"Angel, honey, wake up," she called. Silence greeted Michelle. Trying desperately to calm herself and not alarm Angel, Michelle softly tapped at the door, slowly turning the doorknob at the same time. Michelle's mouth dropped wide open at the sight that met her eyes. Blindly stumbling out of the doorway Michelle raced back down the hallway to awaken Jack.

Rushing into the bedroom, Michelle found Jack sitting up, wide-awake on the side of the bed. Ordinarily Michelle would have questioned his unusually early awakening, but just now she was too frightened and alarmed. Jack's outstretched arms offered a trembling Michelle the comfort and reassurance she needed.

"Baby, what's wrong?"

"It's Angelique!! She's gone and her room is torn apart! I'm afraid something has happened to her!"

"Calm down, baby. Don't jump to conclusions. I'm sure there's a perfectly good answer. You know how kids can be."

As he spoke the reassuring words to Michelle, nestled in his arms, Jack felt an unnerving sense of loss. An unexplainable sense of dread and loss spread over him. Jack couldn't understand his unwarranted feelings, but all he wanted to do now was soothe Michelle, the woman he deeply loved. Placing a false smile on his face Jack hugged Michelle tightly to him and stroked her hair.

"She probably got up early to spend a little quiet time with Paul." The words almost choked in his throat, and a tightness surrounded his heart. He still didn't trust the interloper. All of his misgivings about Paul surfaced, but he had to keep these thoughts from Michelle for now. He would take care of whatever had gone wrong. He vowed to always protect Michelle.

Pulling away, Michelle described the scene that met her eyes, only moments before. On entering Angelique's room Michelle had detected a faint unusual odor. Looking over the disarray on Angelique's dresser Michelle had discovered a message.

"There was a crumpled-up note addressed to you, Jack, smeared in blood! It doesn't make sense!" she screamed hysterically.

Snatching up his robe, Jack raced down the hallway with Michelle at his heels. Quickly they entered Angelique's normally neat bedroom. The message proved not to be written in blood, but rather a watercolor paint. Whoever left the message had a dangerously, diabolically, twisted mind. A cursory check of Angelique's room revealed nothing unusual. The room did look as if someone had hurriedly riffled through Angelique's belongings, but Jack said nothing for the moment. He didn't want to further alarm Michelle.

Jack and Michelle spared no expense in obtaining the best private investigators money could buy. The authorities had been immediately called in, but whoever kidnapped Angelique had been extremely thorough, clever and knowledgeable. It was as if Angelique had never existed. She seemed to have vanished without leaving a trace. Hours turned into days, days into weeks, weeks into months. Little information turned up that hadn't already been uncovered in the first few precious hours after Angelique was discovered missing.

A rescue team had discovered Paul in a frozen ravine a good distance from the clearing he and Angel had been approaching to view the doe and her fawn. Fearing frostbite may have set in, and the possibility of internal injuries, Paul was rushed to the nearest hospital. He had suffered a concussion from a severe blow to his head and was unconscious when found. How Paul had gotten to this area could only be surmised as the powdery snow had all but obliterated any traces of the kidnappers' departure. There was very little information to be learned from him until after his recovery.

The FBI was called in on the apparent kidnapping and determined that the kidnappers had made their escape by using a snowmobile to rendezvous with a helicopter. They deduced that Angelique or Paul had put up a scuffle from the obvious thrashing, evident in the area around the new fallen snow. Angelique's skis had been found near the clearing, along with a very expensive antique silver bracelet with a broken clasp. The origin of the very unusual and intricately styled bangle, the only significant piece of evidence found, still eluded the investigators. To complicate matters further, a linguist was needed to decipher the unusual inscription, worn nearly invisible on the underside of the bracelet.

Many questions surfaced regarding the note discovered on Angelique's dresser which read, "Jack, where is your most prized possession?" It seemed crystal clear to Michelle that a grave mistake had been made. She was sure now that she had been the intended victim, not her Angel. Whoever captured Angelique must have made the same mistake as countless others had. Angelique was a carbon copy of her mother when Michelle was Angelique's age. They both possessed the same bone structure and height. Angelique's difference was in her deeper coloring, which was Jamari's gift to her.

As time dragged on Michelle's nerves wore thin. It was as if her very essence for life was flickering to a close with each passing day. There was little Jack could say or do to console Michelle during this time. One day she was a bundle of hope and positive thinking. The next, she was consumed by guilt for remaining safe. She would have given her very life for the safety of her only child.

"If only the kidnappers would contact us," she prayed.

Feverishly Michelle hoped handwriting analysis would identify the perpetrators, or that the silver bangle could be traced. Nightly she prayed that her daughter would be returned to her whole. Angelique didn't deserve this. Michelle had not spoken to Jamari, Angelique's father, for several years, and regretted having to tell him of their daughter's disappearance. Michelle was taken aback by Jamari's seemingly cool reception to the news. She had not told him in person, and therefore, had not seen the cold fury ignite in his eyes. Jamari may not have been a constant presence in his daughter's life, but he loved her. She was his flesh and blood. Secretly he had always hoped that, at the right time, Angelique would want to get to know him, learn his business, and come live with him. Things had gone drastically wrong! Somehow, he would make them right.

Chapter Six

Deceptions

Josh

The pencil Angelique was savagely gripping in her hand snapped. The sudden harsh sound brought her out of the nightmare she found herself continually re-living. With head bowed over her writing pad Angel forced herself into her new novel. All of her passion was thrown into her writing, which was the catharsis she so desperately needed to ease her pain.

Paul was the first man to disillusion Angelique. She believed he was the one responsible for her spiraling descent into depression, regression and denial.

"No, I can't blame Paul for all my unhappiness," she mused, "but I trusted him, and he betrayed me."

Shoving the notepad aside, Angelique grabbed her sweater from the back of her chair. She couldn't concentrate on her writing. The thought of her chance encounter with Paul Monroe the other day still unnerved her. He was the last person she expected to see when she had contacted the lawyer referral service in her search for an attorney. Angelique had not wanted to use the firm that had handled Michelle and Jack's affairs. She wanted to break free from all persons who reminded her of her loss. Her mother and Jack were gone now too, and Angelique was determined to put her hurt and sorrow behind her.

There were too many questions, expressions of sympathy and sorrow in the eyes of all who knew Angelique. Divorcing Josh had been the easy part. Losing Kimberly, her precious two-year old daughter, so soon after the tragic plane crash that claimed Michelle and Jack, was unbearable.

Angelique blamed herself for Kimberly's death. If she hadn't allowed Josh to pick up Kimberly for a visit with her father, she would be alive today. Angelique knew she couldn't stay in a love-less marriage, but she had not thought that Josh would be so careless with their daughter.

Josh had said all the right things to win her trust. Angelique wasn't looking for a relationship when Josh Sterling appeared on the scene those four long years past. He was very casual in his initial approach to Angelique, yet persistent. Josh was very charismatic, a successful young attorney with the very prestigious Summervale law firm, and the boy wonder when it came to matters involving international law. Josh also came from a very prominent French Moroccan family from the West Coast and was extremely handsome with surfer-boy good looks. Because of their similar cultural and financial backgrounds Angelique didn't feel threatened that he would be out for her money.

Angelique had no idea of who the real Josh was. For a while he was very loving and caring. He convinced Angelique that he was interested in her for the person she was. Josh even feigned ignorance of the connection between the infamous Michelle Dupre and Angelique, even after the recent marriage between Michelle and Jack Montenero had been featured on the front cover of the newspapers and tabloids around the country. Michelle and Jack's union of wealth had been a much-publicized topic.

Josh could not keep up the facade for long, however. Little more than a year and a half into the marriage Angelique discovered the dark side to Josh. He was a brilliant attorney, but his energy and good nature came from the amphetamines he was addicted to. Once they wore off, he was depressed and depressive. It was during one of Josh's down episodes that he revealed to Angelique that he never really cared for her and loving her was out of the question. She was only a trophy to obtain, a mere challenge.

"Love you?" he shouted during one stormy argument, "I don't love you! Your family's money and power are what made me pursue you."

By this time their baby daughter was two months old, and Angelique once more found herself suffocating with the knowledge of being used again by a conniving man. "How could I have been so misled by him?" she thought silently to herself. "At the time Josh seemed so right for me," she said aloud to no one. Jack's intuitive insight in re-writing his and Michelle's wills, and his urging that Angelique legally protect her assets, kept Angelique from being financially indigent. Still, the large settlement Josh received depleted her resources.

Josh had zeroed in on her need to be loved, and to give love. The kidnapping and ensuing ordeal had been hard on Angelique. It was as if everything in the universe had turned upside down. She had felt out of control, and subconsciously wanted a safe haven out of the storms she had been thrown into. She still had no answers for why her island "benefactor" participated in her kidnapping yet was willing to protect her with his very life during her captivity.

Angelique quickly descended the steps leading away from her modest sized townhouse. She had chosen this particular location because of the isolated cul-de-sac, quietness of the area and the nearness of the park. City living had never appealed to Angelique. She had searched relentlessly and finally found the perfect, quiet neighborhood, a safe suburban setting in Alexandria, Virginia in which to nurture Kimberly. Why hadn't Josh kept a better eye on Kimberly as they had crossed a downtown street? Angelique knew the answer to that question. Josh had been too absorbed in making a drug transaction when his baby stepped off the curb and into the path of an oncoming car.

~

Suddenly the impact of the trees dressed in burnt orange and red-gold autumn leaves struck Angelique with a new, raw awareness. Although the trees were shedding their leaves to become barren for the winter, they gracefully accepted their fate. They were not facing death, as Angelique so often longed for, but simply change. How could Angelique face life without her little girl? What reason did she have to carry on?

Angelique's attempt at being civil and reasonable with Josh concerning Kimberly, and a desire for Kimberly to know her father, had motivated Angelique to relinquish the tight rein she kept on Kimmie, as Angel playfully referred to her bundle of energy. Persuasive Josh had taken Kimberly for an afternoon of play. This proved to be the first and last outing for the both of them.

"I'll get past this too!" Angel shouted, with tears streaming down her cheeks. As she aimlessly walked down an old forgotten path in the woods Angelique began to reminisce on her days following her abduction. Tears stung her eyes, but they were healing tears. She had to acknowledge the pain of her ordeals to get past them and begin to live again. She had to recognize and accept the fact that her choices were affected by her attempt to internalize all the horrible things that had happened to her. It was time now to face her life as it was up to this point.

She needed to decide whether to be whole again or be an emotional cripple forever. With labored breathing from the weight of her anxiety, Angelique wrestled with how she could ever truly be safe again. How could she trust anyone else if she couldn't even trust herself? Subconsciously she had chosen the wrong type of men after she had been returned to Michelle. Josh had just been one of a long string of sweet-talking guys after one thing. A challenge.

Angelique had loved her family home, and had returned there briefly after her breakup with Josh. She had hoped to put the thoughts of a failed marriage behind her, and surround Kimmie with the love and attention of her doting grandmother and Jack. But soon after making a new home for she and Kimmie tragedy struck again. A sudden electrical storm arose during Jack and Michelle's returning transatlantic flight, rendering the cockpit's instrument panel inoperative and navigation impossible. Their private plane crashed leaving Angelique grief stricken and in the throes of becoming emotionally unhinged.

After the deaths of Michelle and Jack, the closing of The Chez Paris was inevitable. There were too many memories to haunt Angelique; Michelle's presence could be felt in the very pulse of the boutique. The same was true of each room and corner in the elegant mansion called home. Each room was haunted with the essence of a happier life; at every corner Angelique expected to see her mother's face smiling at her. The healing process could only begin after Angelique freed herself from all reminders.

Silently she walked through the house one last time, memorizing each room and imprinting them forever to memory. The night before she had swept and re-swept each room, remembering the once gleaming hardwood floors of her childhood. She had swept relentlessly, slipping back to a time when joy and laughter were her constant companions. That was before Paul; before the abduction. Desperately she tried to cling to the present memories of her past. But they belonged to a happier era.

This was the second home Angelique had loved and cherished and was compelled to abandon. The third time in her short-lived years she would have to begin again with no direction. Staring at her reflection in the mirror of the downstairs bath Angelique was shocked by what she saw. Her face still possessed a youthful look far younger than her twenty - nine years, and the strain of her ordeals. There were no lines yet about her eyes. Her skin, still taut, held the glow of youth, and her luscious shoulder length auburn hair held no trace of gray.

Chapter Seven

The Dating Game

Whenever Angelique had a rough time, Vivian was always there with a remedy. "Well, I could use a remedy right now," thought Angelique. Before Josh there had been that great relationship with Ray that lasted all of four months. Ray was six foot two, handsome in a rugged way, and slender. "He's too good to be true," Angelique thought at the time, but he finally won her over. He had seemed so thoughtful and sincere, never coming by without bringing her favorite ice cream, or some other small token of affection. Ray and Angel would talk for hours on end about the things that mattered to them both. She had even met his parents and siblings who also seemed to like her.

Ray had pressed home and work phone numbers into her hand as she was leaving the Chez Noir, a popular nightspot in downtown Washington, D.C. At the time Angelique had been celebrating her birthday with Selena, a casual friend, during happy hour. The club that night was filled with quite a number of attractive and seemingly successful men. There were several couples still on the dance floor swaying to the soft jazzy beat of the live reggae band as Angel made her way back to her seat. She had enjoyed a dance and interesting conversation with a very attractive man, when Ray asked her to dance. When she refused, Selena quietly hissed, "He was tall and good looking, and you turned him down?"

"I didn't even look at him," Angel said. "I was too out of breath." Looking into the small crowd of people on the dance floor Angel asked, "Which one is he?"

"Don't stare, but look at the really tall, slim man in the charcoal gray suit near the palm tree."

Adopting a daring spirit from Selena, Angelique began to steadily watch this man until he felt her eyes on him and turned to look directly into her eyes from across the floor. Being bold, Angelique locked eyes with him and them demurely looked down and then up at him again. That invitation cost her some heartache in the long run.

"Why don't you ever have time for me anymore?" Angel asked, after hearing the same old excuse of being "too busy" from Ray. They would talk every day and every evening for hours and see each other during the week and every Friday or Saturday. Until recently. Then he dropped the bomb. Ray had simply forgotten to tell her he already had a ladylove of two years who was pressuring him to make the trip to the altar.

"If you already had someone, why did you even bother with me?" Angelique demanded.

"You looked so good in that black dress, that when I saw you, I couldn't help myself," Ray replied.

"That's just like a man," mused Angel. "Just when you think you have the beginnings of a solid relationship, they throw you a curveball. I'm glad we were never intimate."

Following this fiasco with Ray, Angelique threw herself into her work. She had really begun to care for him, and his confession about his other woman had hurt badly. Angelique had thought Ray might be her future. She had to laugh, though, thinking back on how his son and daughter seemed so confused the one time they all had gotten together for an outing. What pained Angelique the most was the fact that Ray's children seemed to adore her, as she cared for them, from their one shared encounter. "I hope they asked him a million questions about me! He deserves to be put in the hot seat for being so insensitive. Ray had no right to involve his children in his nonsense."

After Ray there had been Andre. He was a sweet biracial man, but he hadn't wanted a ready-made family. Angel could still hear his voice as he formed his lips to say, "Angel, I can deal with you, and I can deal with your child. But I can't handle the two of you together."

"At least he was honest," Vivian had said.

"I could have used a little more honesty up front, before he let me think we had a future together," Angelique had said at the time.

"I know girl," commiserated Vivian, "but at least you found out before you hooked up with him. Just think if you had married that creep."

As usual, Vivian was right again. Vivian and Angelique went back a long way. They had met in high school, had been college roommates for a while, and shared more than just the good times together. Their lives were intimately entwined from shared experiences.

Vivian first met Angelique after her ordeal on the island in the South Pacific. At the time Vivian had been absorbed with the Black Student Union Affairs in the elite private boarding school Michelle had sent Angelique to, on the advice of Angelique's therapist. During their college years Vivian had chaired the Black Student Affairs Committee, and the two worked tirelessly to promote legislation for the homeless. If there was a good cause Vivian was in the midst of it. Not far behind was Angelique.

Although the two girls hailed from different ethnic backgrounds, they had much in common. Vivian had been raised and educated primarily by a multitude of governesses and tutors while her parents pursued their jet-set careers in international law. As an only child she was often isolated from other African Americans due to her parents' foreign travel. As a result she was intent on identifying with and maintaining her African American culture. Angelique, on the other hand, traveled frequently with her mother and Jack, and was also an only child. She had very little contact with her father's obvious African culture and longed to become acquainted with her French Moroccan culture and her father's people.

Angelique and Vivian became inseparable from the start of their friendship at the private school and decided to attend the same college, but with different majors. It was inadvertently through Vivian that Angel met Josh. The Summervales had given a dinner party at their estate during the Christmas break of the girls' last year of undergraduate studies. Josh Sterling attended the dinner party as the new council hired by the Summervale's very prosperous law firm. Vivian unjustly felt responsible for Josh and Angelique meeting, and their resulting marriage, and was determined to stick by her friend after their divorce.

At twenty-eight Vivian was vivacious, dynamic and the best friend and confidant of Angelique. In contrast to Angelique, Vivian stood five feet two with a gorgeous cocoa hued face, an abundance of thick wavy black hair, a lithe, svelte body and the grace and poise of a model. Although the two women had so much going for themselves, they had just not met their long sought for soul mates.

The two friends picked each other up when the times were rough and shared the good times as well. Vivian had her share of bad relationships, and Angelique had been there for her also. The two friends agreed to share more than just man-talk, though, and had forged a solid friendship based on mutual trust. They gave each other space and didn't need to always be in each other's company.

"So how are you and Mr. Leonard getting along?" cooed Angelique while sipping an espresso at SoBe, a trendy Black owned restaurant and lounge in Lanham, Maryland. "Is everything lovey-dovey still between you two?"

"It's going nowhere, and I really don't want to talk about it," Vivian hissed as she sat forlornly folding and unfolding the paper covering of her straw. She held so much nervous energy and frustration inside her that you could almost see the tension knotting the muscles in her neck and shoulders.

"Oops, did I touch a sore spot? So Sorry. But don't snap at me," shrugged Angelique. "The last time I talked to you, you made me think there would be wedding bells soon. What happened?"

"I'm sorry; it's not your fault," Vivian said. "It's just that things were going so good in this relationship. I thought this time I had finally found the right guy. Jamal is sensitive, mature, has an excellent job and career path. He's never expressed any desire to compete with me over money matters. He's not threatened that I have my own business and can pull in big bucks. In short, he's every mother's dream for her daughter. But he's afraid of commitment! I just found out over the weekend that marriage is out of the question, ever. We've been seeing each other for two years now, with no complaints, and he announced he never intends to marry. He's sorry he misled me, but he stills cares! I am so fed up!"

"How did the topic of marriage come up? Did you push too hard?" Angelique asked.

"No. We were actually talking about some friends of his who recently got engaged. When I said they would be a dynamic team together, and any children they have would be lucky, Jamal said that it might work for them, but not him. In all the times we've talked about relationships, etcetera, not once did he discourage me from thinking we would one day have a deeper, closer relationship. It's like he just left that little fact out, 'By the way, marriage is not for me.' I still love him, but I can't stay in a dead-end relationship. I want more than he's willing to give."

The very solicitous Cuban waiter who had enthusiastically greeted Vivian and Angelique was instantly beside their table. He moved as silently and swiftly as a cat about to pounce on its' prey. "Are you ready to order now?" he inquired. Vivian, who had appeared disinterested in food until this moment, began to rattle off a list of fattening goodies she wanted to sample.

"Hold on, Viv," chided Angel, "let's not put on an extra twenty pounds to celebrate. You'll regret it when you look in the mirror."

"You keep me centered," Vivian stated honestly." To the waiter, who stood nonchalantly at her elbow listening to the exchange, Vivian adopted a bright smile and replied, "Scratch the first order; I'll have the scallops marinated in wine sauce, a Caesar salad, and a refill on the iced tea." Angelique quickly gave her order of shrimp salad Creole and corn chowder and opted too for an iced tea to cool her throat from the zesty Cajun spices. Noting his trim build as the waiter walked away, Angelique slowly exhaled. She had a story of her own to tell, and perhaps by sharing it, it wouldn't feel so bad.

"Listen, Vivian, I know how you feel. I know several other women who say the same things. The men are either too young and with hang ups, have part time jobs and no aspirations, underpaying or no jobs at all and want someone to take care of them. And let's not forget the men who measure our worth by how much *we* can help them. It's sad, but finding a good man complete in himself is like trying to find a dinosaur. They're extinct." With that said Vivian and Angelique shared a bittersweet, knowing laugh.

"If it makes you feel any better," Angel said, "think back on my brief but painful experience with Michael from Atlanta." Angelique had met him on a business trip through an associate.

"My mind was on the business that had brought me to Atlanta, and I just wasn't interested in meeting a new man and getting my hopes up, only to be disappointed again. My mind was on anything else but getting to know this man. In fact, I didn't pay him any attention when he came by the hotel suite. That's probably why he tried so hard…at first."

"Do you remember Glenda, my co-worker at the time?" Angel asked.

"Well, I was working for the Bureau then, and they had set the two of us up in a suite to save money. Two separate rooms were too expensive, they said. The cheapskates! Anyway, Glenda invited Anjare, a friend of hers living in Atlanta, to stop by while we were in town. Michael was with him. Glenda claims Anjare didn't mention bringing a friend with him. I just ignored Michael and that must have piqued his interest."

"I can't believe you did that," replied Vivian.

"Believe it," Angel replied. "I didn't even change from the slouchy sweatpants and mismatched tee shirt I had changed into after my flight. You know me, I slammed whatever was available into my overnight bag that would be comfy." Angel had to smile at the remembered episode.

"So how did things go wrong?" Vivian asked.

"During his visit I was so aloof! When he gave me his card with his phone number, I didn't volunteer mine."

"You know you had him going now;" Vivian replied, "no man wants to think you aren't interested in him. It's an ego thing."

"So True. Anyway, as the evening progressed, we chatted amiably enough. The four of us ate a simple dinner in our suite; I wasn't interested in going out with them. Michael was in heaven; he had mentioned earlier that he was to meet someone for cocktails later on that evening, but he just wouldn't leave."

"Stop it!" Vivian cried. "It must be true! If you dog a man, he loves you for it! Why can't I dog a man I'm truly interested in? I might get more staying power."

"Do you want to hear the rest of this?" interjected Angelique.

"Of course I do! I'm all ears."

Angel continued, "You would have thought Michael had hit the lottery! He couldn't remove the smile he had plastered on his face!" Vivian was in tears now from laughter; it wasn't funny, but Angel's re-telling was so vivid and dramatic.

"I refused his invitation to go out, preferring to get some sleep. When he was finally ready to leave, I asked him if he was still going to meet his friend - the man was dressed in a very elegant charcoal grey Armani suit and tie - and I must admit, the man did look good! Well, do you know he had completely forgotten all about this woman and the evening they had planned?"

"Oooh," cried Vivian, "you must have been devastating! What happened to that honey?"

"The same thing that happens whenever you let a man know you're interested," replied Angelique. "They suddenly start feeling trapped. You'd think we women had neon signs saying, *I want to get married* imprinted on our foreheads." At this point Angelique sighed heavily. "Who's to say what went wrong," she replied, with disappointment tingeing her words. "I just know that after an attempt latter on, on my part, for a possible connection, there was a short circuit. Distance didn't help much either. End of story."

What Angel did not reveal to Vivian was her brief relationship to Ian Stone, a man a few years younger than Angel. Age did not matter, he kept repeating to Angel's refusal to take him seriously. After much protesting on Angel's part, Ian wore her down. She began to believe that maybe Ian was different. Maybe he really was interested in her, the person. He seemed to be a spiritual person by all outward displays and conversation. Finally Angel reached out to Ian. After the nightmare of Josh, Angel decided to make a grasp at the prospect of having someone to share her dreams, someone to love, and to love her in return.

It had been so very long since she had felt the stirrings of longing and desire. Those feelings had been so deeply submerged for years. Angel was shocked by their abrupt re-emergence. She had been on guard for the advances of men she knew or those she assumed to be on the prowl. Angel was on guard from men she knew, and strangers alike. She had incorrectly determined that Ian was different because he wasn't a stranger. And he was so convincing.

Angelique had known of Ian Stone for years, and they both were board members of the same non-profit charitable organization. Ian carried himself in such a positive manner. Many of his friends and associates were of high moral standing, and on this fact, Angel judged Ian to be a good and safe man. His lips were soft. His warm breath on her neck and shoulders, and the caresses from his strong hands sent her mind reeling with an ecstasy she couldn't have imagined. Yet Angel resisted his advances on their first encounter. She was not ready for him and couldn't fathom a sensual or sexual interlude with this quiet young man, or any man for that matter. Angel had been deeply hurt by Josh's rejection years before, and by the games of the men she had met in the years following her divorce from Josh.

But it was too late. Angel had been caught off guard and so she had unwittingly opened the door to suffering again. Throughout the night after Ian had left Angel could still feel his lips on her tingling skin. His hands had caressed her everywhere, setting her on fire. While her lips said no her body longed for fulfillment. Hours after their brief time together she could still feel the pressure of his sinewy limbs entangled in hers. As he softly caressed her, her mind screamed in confusion.

Thus began Angel's journey again in disappointment. It didn't take long. As Angel became enraptured, Ian pulled away. Once he sought her out, now he seemed indifferent. Although Angel had been a married woman, she had no skills for the diabolical game Ian played. He had been the hunter, and after he had captured his *prize* he was no longer interested. Even though Angel confided in Vivian, her best friend, she was not about to reveal this latest hurt. It was too new and painful.

"Listen," Vivian said, as she tossed the crumpled napkin into her now empty plate. "It's Thursday. The week is almost over. Let's get together real soon and work up some steam and purge these men from our systems. My shoulders are getting heavy from carrying these feelings around all day."

"That sounds good to me," Angel replied as she placed a few bills on the check. "This time it's on me.

The shrill ring of the telephone woke Angelique from a sound sleep. The clock on her wicker bedside table showed 7:30. Books and papers went flying as Angel groped for the cell phone to stop the jarring ring. Who could be calling this early on a Saturday morning?

"Hello," she mumbled into the phone.

"Hey girl, wake up," came the bubbly voice of Vivian Summervale on the other end of the line. "Join me at the spa for a workout and quick brunch afterwards at the pancake house."

Vivian was a school administrator turned entrepreneur. She had started her own consulting firm two years ago on a shoestring after years of frustration with school bureaucracy.

"Listen, I haven't had much sleep," Angel rasped, "give me a rain check."

"No way! You've been moping around too long. I'll see you at 9:30 in the gym." The perceptible click signaled the end of that conversation.

"What nerve!" grumbled Angelique as she threw back her covers and headed for the shower. The tingling spray of hot water followed by cool was just what Angel needed to revive her. She had had a restless night as usual after dwelling on the unhappy details of her life after the kidnapping.

I'm going to give miss know-it-all a piece of my mind when I see her," Angel grumbled. She knew Vivian was right on target. That girl seemed to have a sixth sense when it came to timing. Just recently Angelique had met a man whom she had been immediately attracted to. He seemed to share her feelings too, but lately he had begun shying away, never having any time for the two of them to get together.

"Well, I've got no more time to worry over that man or any other," Angel said to herself. "If I don't hurry, I'll be late, and I don't want to hear *Miss Thang's* mouth." Angelique was smiling and humming a soulful Jill Scott tune. She was really looking forward to seeing Vivian and was way overdue for a workout at the gym. They first started working out when Kimmie was four months old. The two friends would dash over to the gym leaving Kimmie in the capable hands of a staff volunteer who would sit just outside the door of their aerobics class. It was hard going back to the gym those first few times after Kimmie's accident. Everyone had been so kind, but the retelling to people who hadn't known of Kimmie's accident was the hardest.

Chapter Eight

Manipulations

Amelia

Had the nurse posted at Paul's bedside heard correctly? There it was again, the almost imperceptible whisper. Rising quickly, Amelia leaned over her patient, listening and staring intently, for some sign of arousal. Paul had been unconscious for three days now.

Angel, Angel, softly escaped his bruised, full lips. Yes, Amelia had heard correctly. Instantly she sent an alert for the attending physician. She had been instructed to notify her in the event of any change. There was great concern over Paul's head injury. Permanent damage could not be ruled out until he awoke from his body's supposedly healing sleep. Everyone, including the police, was anxiously awaiting the moment he could be questioned.

Amelia had spent an inordinate amount of time with this particular patient. She was well schooled in not becoming too attached to a patient, but she was immediately attracted to Paul after one glance at his inert form the evening he was brought in. More than once she had sat past her appointed time, hoping she would be the first person Paul saw when he awoke. He was a classically handsome young man, not much younger than her twenty-two years. To Amelia's chagrin, it had not gone undetected, either, that the first sound coming from her patient was the name of a woman!

The details surrounding Paul's head trauma were unknown to Amelia. Her curiosity was piqued by the obviously official persons who hovered nearby, awaiting Paul's awakening. Even more intriguing was the guard that had been posted outside his door from the moment he was brought in. Paul hardly looked the criminal type but looks could be deceiving. Amelia wondered if she could keep an ethical distance if he showed any interest in her.

"Angel," he croaked loudly. "Where is Angel? Where am I?"

"It's alright," Amelia soothed. "You've had an accident; you're in the hospital. The doctor will be here in a moment. Please try to be calm."

Noting the fear in Paul's eyes, Amelia continued, holding his right hand, "My name is Amelia; I'm your nurse and I'll be right here if you need anything."

"I can't see!" implored Paul.

"You sustained a blow to the head," Amelia explained. "Let Doctor Barnes examine you. She will be here very soon. Just try to be calm."

The sight of Dr. Judith Barnes coming through the door was a relief to Amelia. Paul was becoming increasingly agitated and Amelia feared he might go into shock. Her professional detachment was slipping; she was in serious jeopardy of becoming too involved.

"Let's have a look at you," came the doctor's brisk response. The doctor's presence seemed to have a calming effect on Paul. He lay back on his pillows, quiet for the time being.

"I'm Dr. Judith Barnes, chief of Neurosurgery; can you tell me how you're feeling?"

"My head hurts; I feel like a train ran over me, and I can't see."

Doctor Barnes shot a quick glance at Amelia who quickly nodded.

Let me check you thoroughly and run some tests. Don't be alarmed at your vision loss. It may be temporary. You sustained quite a blow to your head." With that said Judith Barnes ordered the necessary tests, gave further instructions, and inquired of Paul's parents. The doctor learned that his mother had died when he was young, and that his father was out of the country. What a horrible time to be all alone. Upon hearing this Amelia was more determined now than ever to give her charge extra care.

The authorities insisted on speaking with Paul, but they were only allowed a few moments in his room. The most important thing now was for Paul to rest and begin to heal. Since Paul had no family present, Michelle and Jack visited with him to keep up his spirits. At the moment they were being very supportive of him, while anxiously trying to uncover the mystery surrounding Angelique's disappearance. They still did not know if Paul had been instrumental in her kidnapping. They also did not want to leave the area and return home until some contact had been made by the kidnappers.

After a thorough examination Paul received a promising prognosis, although for the time being, he had no sight. As time passed, he began to rely on Amelia to keep him connected to the outside world. She began coming to Paul's room frequently to read the online news to him and keep him informed of the search for Angelique. Paul confided to Amelia who Angelique was, and how much she meant to him. He was outwardly distraught that he could not be of much help concerning Angel's abduction. Paul only remembered that he had been grabbed from behind and administered the savage blow on the head when he began to struggle.

As time passed Paul began to regain his sight slowly. His recovery would be a long, slow process, but he would suffer no lasting physical effects. Amelia began to care for Paul more and more each day. She tried desperately to keep her feelings to herself because she knew Paul did not feel the same way about her. In a possessive way Amelia began to take note of all visitors to Paul's room. During his convalescence she couldn't help but notice a visitor who had come several times before, but who now left his room in tears; a strikingly attractive young woman whom Paul had been very closed mouthed about.

Noting the sorrow and distress on Paul's face following the departure of his visitor, Amelia took this opportunity to subtly find out who this woman was. Entering his room after softly knocking, Amelia presented Paul with her most radiant smile.

"How's my favorite patient today?" she quipped. "Is there anything I can get you? Some juice or a magazine?"

"No, I'm okay," muttered Paul desolately.

"Say, you don't seem your usual self...is something wrong?"

Reaching for the bedside buzzer Amelia continued, "Do you need me to call the doctor for you?" She hoped the comment would elicit more conversation from Paul, and it did have the desired effect.

"No, don't call for the doctor," Paul protested, "I feel okay. I just had to take care of something unpleasant that should have been done long ago."

This was the opening Amelia had been waiting for. "Paul, I don't want to pry," she began, "but would you like to talk about it? I can see now that your visitor upset you. Did you receive bad news about your missing friend?" Amelia was almost one hundred percent sure that the attractive woman had not brought news of Paul's missing lady. Tears on the woman's face in departure had replaced her cheerful countenance on her arrival. And that spoke volumes. Whatever their conversation had been about, Amelia was determined to find out all she could in the hopes of getting closer to Paul. At this very moment Paul was extremely vulnerable, and Amelia was in the right place at the right time, offering warmth and understanding.

"Monique is someone very close to me," Paul began, "someone who's always been there for me. We go back a long way.

We always talked of becoming engaged to be married, but under the circumstances, I can't go through with a marriage."

"But Paul," Amelia soothingly began, "you are improving with each day; you don't have any serious injuries and your sight should return to normal in time." Hoping Paul would take the bait, Amelia almost held her breath in anticipation of Paul's next words.

"It isn't my health that's holding me back," Paul explained, "my heart belongs to someone else now." Looking down at his covers and looking every bit as miserable as Monique had, Paul continued. "I just hurt a truly wonderful person. I feel so bad for hurting Monique, but I couldn't keep up the pretense any longer."

A light tapping on the hospital door preceded the lieutenant's entrance and ended Amelia's sleuthing into Paul's affairs. She excused herself, leaving Paul alone with the detectives. "Sorry to bother you, but we need to ask a few more questions. I'm Lt. Arnold; we talked earlier. And this is Officer Wayne. We'll try to be brief, but we need you to recount everything that happened the morning Miss Dupre was abducted."

On and on the questioning went for several hours. It was as if they didn't believe his story. But Paul had nothing to hide. Not really. It was true. Jack Montenero and Paul's mother, Serita, had a business relationship several years back. But that was before she had met and married his father. It didn't seem important to mention it at the time. If he were to suddenly reveal it now, it would appear that he had been deliberately trying to hide something.

Paul was extremely confused and distraught. He felt that somehow, he must be responsible for Angelique's disappearance, but he didn't know what to do. Just before Spring break he had contacted Raphael Medici, his godfather and one of his mother's former business contacts, in the hopes of obtaining work during his vacation. His father was out of the country at the time, and Paul was trying to be self-reliant. Raphael had always told Paul to call on him if he ever needed anything. Each holiday over the years brought a card with a monetary gift, although Paul had not seen Raphael since he was very young. Paul assumed it had something to do with his father since Mr. Monroe had very little to say whenever Raphael's name came up.

Talking aloud to convince himself, Paul felt his chest tighten with the dawning of realization. "Raphael Medici was the one who made the position available for me at the ski chalet. I still remember being told there was no work until I mentioned Raphael's name."

The three employees behind the desk had suddenly stopped what they were doing and looked furtively at one another, and then quickly at Paul before resuming their tasks. Joe, the manager, too seemed shaken but recovered quickly saying, "Oh...yeah...we do need an extra man to help with the ski rental equipment and the snack bar." Paul quickly agreed to the very generous salary offered him. Snapping his fingers, Joe gestured to one of his help to show Paul where he could get settled in for the next few weeks.

"So you know Raphael Medici, eh?" Joe asked.

"Yes, he's my godfather," Paul said, straightening up under the heavy backpack he slung over his shoulders. Joe's expression revealed he was startled, but he said nothing as he watched Paul's retreating back. Thinking back on this incident caused Paul to raise some serious questions about Raphael Medici, his possible connections to Angelique's disappearance, and whether he, Paul, had unwittingly been a pawn in her abduction. Covering his face with his hands Paul moaned softly, "Angel...Angel."

Raphael - Serita

Raphael Medici was a shrewd businessman who remembered every injustice, real or imagined. His loyalty to those who were fair to him, and to those he held affection for, ran deep. So too ran his thirst for revenge. Kyle Monroe, Paul's father, never said much on the subject of Raphael with good reason. Even though he had no proof, Kyle believed Raphael had been secretly in love with Paul's mother, Serita, for years, before she had met and married Kyle. Their meeting had been purely accidental, and Kyle could remember it as if it had happened yesterday.

It was during the rainy season in May, in the city of Puerto Limon, Costa Rica where fate dealt a winning hand to Kyle. He had taken a brief trip there to rest and rejuvenate after a particularly strenuous tour of duty, which had carried him to Nicaragua. Kyle had chosen this particular spot because English was spoken here too, and his travel time would be limited by his close proximity to his base of operation.

Kyle had been traveling on a section of the four hundred and nine mile Inter-American Highway that links Nicaragua to Costa Rica when a sudden downpour made the road treacherous. Just ahead of him he noticed a car pulled off on the shoulder of the road. Kyle had considered pushing on, but visibility was almost impossible. He pulled off the road behind the other car and waited until the rain lessened in severity. Inside the other parked car, which needed a tire change, was Serita Rodriguez. When the rain slacked up Serita frantically ran to the car parked behind hers hoping to get help changing the flat tire. She was returning from an exhaustive meeting, which Jack Montenero had insisted upon, concerning her and Raphael's export business. Kyle helped Serita with her car and followed her into Puerto Limon, an important port on the Caribbean Sea, through which the bulk of the nation's exports pass.

"I insist on following you into the city to make sure you arrive safely," Kyle stated.

"That's very nice of you," demurred Serita in a husky voice, "but I'm sure I'll be alright. I've imposed on you enough for one evening."

Kyle wanted to make sure Serita would arrive safely, but he was also intrigued by this exotic looking fragile woman. The remainder of his brief respite was spent falling in love with the beautiful brown-eyed woman with the generous smile and fire dancing in her eyes.

Raphael never forgave Jack for insisting on the late evening meeting. A meeting which he refused to attend, and which inadvertently introduced Serita to Kyle, the man who would take her away from Raphael. He vowed silently to one day pay Jack back for his misfortune.

Chapter Nine

Reunion

To come face to face with Paul after what seemed an eternity shook Angelique to her very core. This was a man she could no more resist than she could resist her next intake of breath. She was truly tempted, and though she asked for strength, her resolve weakened. She was human, and she fiercely wanted Paul. "How can I feel this way?" she gasped. Angel was no longer the naïve teen she had been when they first met. Now she was a fully-grown woman who had experienced more than her fair share of what life throws at you. "I wanted to be in his arms enjoying his masculinity once more."

The flesh is weak, although the mind is strong. Deep down inside Angelique's intellect said, *No, stay away from him.* No echoed in her thoughts while a yielding, resounding *Yes!* screamed in her limbs. Like a moth is drawn to a flame, so too was Angel drawn to Paul...to be ultimately devoured? "How could I have been so foolish? How could I believe Paul when he said he had tried to help me that disastrous day I was kidnapped?"

Thoughts of Paul Monroe stayed with Angelique throughout her misery on the island. Paul had gotten inside her head and heart, and no amount of rebuking him would erase him from her memory. After her rescue Angel had questioned her mother, Jack and her father, Jamari. All of them advised her to forget Paul in the hopes that she would. Jamari had been kinder to her questions about Paul, but none of them thought Paul was someone who would be good for her. They believed he would be a constant reminder of her pain on the island, and a source of discontent. They were wrong.

Inhaling deeply, Angelique forced oxygen into her lungs to stave off an anxiety attack, while willing herself to get control of her emotions. Seeing Paul at her recent book signing had taken every ounce of control she could gather to keep herself from bolting like a wild animal. Instead, Angelique had turned to the manager of the bookstore and calmly offered an excuse for her hasty departure. After leaving a generous number of signed copies of her latest best seller for distribution, Angel quickly glanced once more at Paul standing outside the storefront. He had become agitated when he realized what was happening inside. Their eyes met and Angelique was horrified at the mixture of longing and fear that crept over her.

Snatching up her purse Angelique made a hasty retreat through the back of the establishment. With purposeful strides Angel practically lunged at her car, willing herself inside before there could be any confrontation. Sensing her direction of flight, Paul circled the building and was waiting in apprehension and anticipation for this reunion.

"Angel, don't be afraid," came a husky male voice over her shoulder. The deep, soft texture of the voice startled yet pleased Angel all at once. Turning sharply, Angelique found herself face to face with Paul, her first love and the person she held responsible for her abduction. Angelique's face shone with pleasure mingled with the confusing mixed emotions she had kept bottled up for so many years. All of her apprehensions slipped away one by one as she gazed into his eyes. Checking herself abruptly, her jaw muscles clenched involuntarily. The warmth in her eyes was slowly replaced by a piercing look of wariness.

"Why are you here?" she demanded. There was no friendliness in her tone.

"I've been trying to find you for years," Paul replied. "You've got to understand..."

Angel cut him off. "Yes, I understand. You used me to get at Jack and my mother. You caused me so much pain!" She turned her back to Paul so he wouldn't witness the tears forming in her eyes. She also hoped he didn't hear the catch in her throat as she spat the venomous accusation at him. With her back still to Paul she softly uttered the final blow, "I believed I loved you once."

Her use of the past tense jarred Paul to the reality of their situation. How could he expect Angel to feel the same for him after so many years? And it was quite evident she held him responsible for her kidnapping. He let his mind momentarily go adrift with his thoughts,

thoughts of how he would find his Angel and recapture the feelings they once shared for one another. Paul now knew it would be a battle to win back her trust.

"Angel, I won't say I understand all that you've been through," Paul croaked, trying to penetrate the invisible protective shell Angelique had erected around herself. "But you must believe me when I say I did not set you up. I was a pawn just as you were!"

With eyes flashing dangerously, Angelique turned the full force of her fury on Paul. "Oh, I guess I'm supposed to just believe you because you say so! My whole being - mental and physical - was invaded, degraded and abused. You were the link. You made it all possible!"

"That's not true!" Paul cried, but Angel cut him off.

"Because of you, everything I hear, touch or see is through the eyes of that long-ago hostage. You've tainted every experience I have ever had from that hideous moment on. You may not have physically killed my little daughter, but if that time had never been, I would still have my baby today!!" Angel spat at Paul.

Realizing Angelique was fast losing control of herself, Paul quickly backed away. He realized his appearance was too sudden, but what should he have done? Somehow, he had to break through her tough exterior and make her understand he had no knowledge of the evil that had been plotted so long ago.

Pulling a card from his pocket, Paul quickly scribbled his home phone number on the back and extended the card to Angelique, who peered at him in horror.

"I'm sorry for everything, but you're completely wrong about me."

Seeing that Angel wouldn't accept his card, Paul placed it under the windshield wiper on her car.

"When you're able to hear the truth call me," Paul replied. "No matter what time, I'll be there for you. I still love you," he said in parting.

Angelique dissolved into tears as she stared at Paul's retreating back. One part of her wanted to call out to him; the other part wanted him to suffer as she had. To feel the desolation that had crept into her heart allowing no warmth, the albatross that sat on her shoulder from morning to night taunting her for her misguided love. For some inexplicable reason Angel hesitated momentarily before snatching the card from her windshield. Initially she had every intention of tearing it up. But she hesitated for just a moment, and in that moment, she made her decision. The only word she uttered was *vengeance* as she slipped the crumpled card into her purse.

Paul was stunned by the change in Angel. Gone was the warmth and calm he remembered in the Angelique he had met years ago. The woman who had stood before him was wound tight and about to explode. "I should have known better than to just appear at the book signing out of nowhere. What was I thinking?" he muttered as he found himself in his selenite grey metallic Mercedes Benz driving aimlessly along the parkway.

There was a coolness in the evening air as Paul replayed the bizarre scene that had just taken place between he and Angelique. This coolness was in sharp contrast to the heated exchange that he had just been involved in. Realization hit hard. Paul now knew it would be extremely difficult, if not impossible, to regain Angelique's trust and love. He had hoped their reunion would have been smoother. Their separation had been far too long. He felt powerless in not knowing what Angel had gone through during her period of abduction and cursed himself for not being able to locate her sooner. He simply had not had unlimited resources for private investigators.

Suddenly looking at his clenched fists, Paul realized how tightly he had been gripping the steering wheel. His creamy, smooth mellow-toned skin, which had taken on a sizzling golden bronze hue from the warming effects of the sun, was blanched pale around his knuckles from the intensity of his grip on the wheel. Willing himself to relax, Paul slowed at the approaching exit ramp, pulling off into Haines Point, a park in Washington, D.C. He had been driving aimlessly and hadn't even realized how far he had driven from the book signing in Georgetown.

Paul brought his Benz to a stop under a deliciously scented flowering cherry blossom tree along the basin of the Potomac River. He had an urgent need to dispel the tension that had built up in him after this last encounter with Angelique. From the trunk of his car Paul removed the athletic gear he kept stashed there for impromptu sessions on a basketball or tennis court. As he strolled under the waning sun, he made his way to the tennis courts to work out his mounting tension. After a brief but brisk set he opted to merely walk and let the remaining tension slowly evaporate. Coming upon *The Awakening*, a statue which arises from the earth depicting man's birth from clay, Paul felt that it was time for a re-birth of sorts for himself and Angelique.

"I need to take a different approach with my Angel," he muttered. "This time I'll get her attention first and let her be willing to come to me." With that thought Paul began a light jog back to his car. It was getting near dusk, time to leave the park and his troubles behind. It was time to put into action his new plan. For the first time Paul became aware of the majesty of the surrounding lushness of the park, redolent in all its colorful glory.

~

"I can't put this off any longer," thought Angel. "It's time to do some housekeeping with my financial affairs." It was seven - thirty on a Tuesday morning. Selecting her favorite jazz station on the radio, Angel began humming a tranquil melody as she selected sandalwood scented beads for her bath. She would start the day with a relaxing, luxurious bath, fortify herself with a sumptuous yet healthy breakfast and meet with an attorney at Tate & Marlborough, a law firm in Silver

Spring, Maryland she had been considering putting on a retainer. "Today I pamper myself," mused Angelique, as she wrapped a large fluffy towel around her body and wound another smaller towel turban-style around her still damp locks. "I've been on edge lately, but no more."

Angelique sat at her vanity smoothing sandalwood and aloe lotion over her body from head to toe. After applying a skin freshener and moisturizer to her face she smoothed a hint of shadow over her eyelids, glossed her luscious lips with cherry bronze lip balm and brushed a hint of blush over her cheeks. Her lashes were long, thick and curly and needed no attention. Next Angel swept her hair off her face and into a French braid for drama. Wispy tendrils of curls framed her delicate face making her appear elegant and sophisticated. After applying a fresh coat of matching cherry bronze polish to her already manicured and pedicured nails, Angelique sat back contentedly to let them dry. She had already selected a cream-colored linen pantsuit trimmed in ivory lace and a short-sleeved round neck silk blouse in a muted hue of cherry bronze to compliment her look.

Now that spring had arrived, and the weather had finally turned warm, Angelique was more than ready to shed her darker, heavier winter colors. Sliding her diminutive size 6 feet into a pair of open toed sandals, Angelique took one last look in the mirror. With a satisfied smile she scooped up the keys to her Porsche for the forty-five-minute drive to her early afternoon appointment.

"Good morning," murmured the receptionist. "May I help you?"

"Yes. I'm Mrs. Josh Sterling and I have an 11:30 appointment."

"Please have a seat. I'll let Mr. Tate know you are here. He asked me to ring him as soon as you arrived."

"Thank you," Angelique replied, and turned to settle herself in a comfortable chair. Moments later she was told there would be a small delay. "Mr. Tate apologizes, but an emergency has come up. He must leave immediately." Speaking in a perfectly modulated voice as if to sooth a cranky child, the receptionist continued, "I've been instructed to tell you that Mr. Tate has arranged for Mr. Monroe, one of our new and extremely competent partners, to speak with you if that meets with your approval."

"Yes, that will be fine," Angelique, stated after deliberating for a moment. With an audible sigh of relief the receptionist ushered Angelique through the massive wooden doors, down a winding hallway with a turn to the left and right, to finally settle her in a small but comfortable conference room. Declining a refreshment, Angelique became caught up in the room's appointments. A circular oak table stood in the middle of the room flanked by matching chairs upholstered in a luminous, dark blue fabric.

A small buffet sat along the backside of the wall with coffee or tea to be consumed in delicate gold-rimmed cups and saucers. The wall facing the hallway was made entirely of glass. Angelique imagined it was to dispel the feeling of claustrophobia, as there was no window in this chamber. Interrupting her thoughts, the efficient receptionist cleared her throat, gave Angelique a slight smile and excused herself saying she would give Mr. Monroe the folder with the particulars she had gathered from Angelique over the phone.

Mr. Monroe's morning had just been cleared, and because he had been free, he agreed to see Alan Tate's client, Mrs. Josh Sterling, as a favor. Normally he would have declined but his caseload was light. He had just successfully closed several trying cases and had time on his hands. As the esteemed Mr. Monroe strode purposefully down the hall from his office his eyes fastened on the petite woman sitting in the glass enclosed conference room, better known as the fishbowl. Her back was to him, but there was something very familiar about her silhouette, the way she held her head. Was the lighting playing a trick on his eyes he wondered?

Coming closer, yet several feet away still, the realization of who Mrs. Sterling was dawned on the esteemed Mr. Monroe. Here sat the woman he had been searching for, for more years than he cared to admit. Hearing a muted tread on the plush carpet, Angelique turned slightly to the sound of the footsteps. Their eyes met. Shock, replaced by panic, shone in Angelique's eyes as she woodenly rose from her chair. Furtively she looked around for some means of escape. There was none. There was only one way in and one way out of the conference room. And a somewhat older Paul Monroe now blocked that exit.

Clutching her purse in her hands Angelique managed to give a slight nod to Paul's solemn greeting. They were both shocked at seeing one another. All sound had frozen in Angelique's throat, but Paul hadn't seemed to notice. Pulling herself together, Angel was the one to speak first.

"I had no idea you were with this law firm."

"I've been on board a little over three years," Paul replied.

"I'm afraid I won't be doing business with your firm," Angelique nervously stated. "If you will excuse me, I won't take up anymore of your valuable time."

Paul reached out and clasped Angelique's free hand in his. An electric current seemed to run through his fingertips to hers. They both felt the tingling sensation, and Angelique quickly removed her hand from Paul's. An urgency came over Paul to have her stay. She was like a frightened doe in a forest that had stumbled on an encampment of humans. Looking at her he realized she still held captive a part of him. He longed to take her in his arms and calm her fears. Angelique's next remark brought Paul out of his reverie. He had drifted back in time to his encounter with her so many years ago when they both had been enchanted with one another.

"If you will excuse me," Angelique said once more with irritation in her voice, "I would like to leave. I do not wish to do business with you now or ever." With that said Angelique brushed past Paul, leaving him with a million questions. Why was she still so obviously angry with him? He would have to get to the bottom of this.

Paul was more shocked now than he had been last Tuesday. After a fruitless ten-year search Angelique had simply sauntered into the law firm of Tate & Marlborough exuding an air of supreme confidence. Angel hadn't noticed the tall young man observing her at a distance discreetly from a corner office. She was radiantly gorgeous and commanded the eyes and attention of all around her. Little did he know then that this was a facade, an appearance as precarious as a house of cards that would topple with the slightest disturbance. The same question kept playing through his head now as it had last Tuesday, "Why is Angelique so angry with me?" He hadn't done anything wrong then or now, or had he?

Chapter Ten

The Mating Call

The insistent ring of the doorbell jarred Angelique awake. "What now?" she muttered, "I'm not up for company after the fiasco with Paul at Mystery Books and the law firm." Peeping through the mini blinds from her upstairs bedroom window Angelique made out the outline of a small van with bright lettering on its side. From this vantage point she couldn't make out the logo. Padding quickly down the stairs more than a little irritated, she opened the door to a breathtaking floral display.

"Mrs. Angelique Sterling?" queried the voice behind the effusive arrangement.

"Yes...yes I'm Angelique Sterling," Angel managed to rasp out as she took in the magnificent display of exotic tropical blooms. It took a moment for Angel to regain her voice. "Who sent these?" she asked, with incredulity in her voice. "There must be some mistake." The driver indicated a card tucked inside the arrangement.

As the truck sped away into the night Angelique wearily reclined against the now closed door. A sigh escaped her lips as she gazed in awe at the massive arrangement, all the while drinking in the heady perfume that assailed her senses. Across the card in a bold script was written, "To a very beautiful lady. These blooms pale beside you." The card was simply signed *M.* Angelique searched her memory but could not put a name or face to the mysterious *M.*

"Maybe in the morning this will make sense," she said out loud to no one. Hugging her rose patterned silk robe to her, Angelique ascended the stairs feeling somewhat refreshed, even though she had no hint as to the identity of her secret admirer. The flowers brightened her otherwise somber mood. Paul Monroe dredged up thoughts and emotions Angelique thought she had long ago buried.

A quiet and peaceful spring shower ushered in the morning. The air was resplendent with the earthy fragrance of freshly mown grass and honeysuckle, mingled with the bouquet Angelique received the night before. Fortified with a light breakfast of carrot cake muffins and hot herbal tea Angelique settled herself in her den with the arduous task of editing a manuscript she had just completed. The really hard work began with this process. Although she had several persons to proofread and edit her work, Angelique actually took pleasure in reliving each of her novels in this fashion. Pushing aside all other thoughts, Angel threw herself into the task. The soft peal of her door chime brought Angelique back to the present.

"I should be used to being stood up by now," chided Vivian as she made a graceful entrance wearing a sleek black catsuit and burnished gold colored leather sandals. A floral sarong skirt was tied around her slim hips emphasizing her tiny waist. "Don't tell me you forgot the plans we made for today?"

"I'm sorry," apologized Angelique. "My mind has been on other things lately."

"I know how that can be," commiserated Vivian, "but it's after 2:00, and by the looks of you, I'll bet you haven't even stopped to eat."

Accepting no excuses, Vivian herded Angelique to her master suite to select an outfit perfect for the park. "I've got a picnic basket of sandwiches, fruit, salad and chilled white wine calling your name," Vivian saucily quipped over her shoulder as she then made her way to Angelique's kitchen. "Now you do have to eat, and I forgot to pack utensils. So how about a truce?   We'll be gone two hours max. Besides, I really need to talk." This stopped all Angelique's protests. What was a friendship for if you didn't nurture it by making time for your friend?

"You win this time, Vivian. I really am hungry and could use a break."

Soon the duo was ready with Angelique in a pair of snug fitting denim blue jeans, crimson bodysuit and cream-colored knit sweater tied around her hips. A pair of white sneakers completed her look.

"Can I help you?" Vivian blurted out as she opened the door to stare into the startled face of a bicycle courier, with hand poised to ring the bell.

"I've got a delivery for a Mrs. Sterling."

"That's me. Where do I sign?" replied Angelique, thinking this was a package from her publisher. To her surprise the man produced a slim silver box. Noting the hesitancy and confusion on her friend's face, Vivian rescued the moment by signing for the package as Angelique looked on spellbound. After shutting the door Vivian turned to her friend with a worried look.

"What's wrong? You look as if you've seen a ghost?"

"It's nothing. I was expecting something else, that's all."

"Well, let's have a look. The box is pretty, but what's inside has got to be more interesting."

A pale peach colored rose emerged from the wrappings, complete with a note in the same bold script as the one the night before. "You are like the petals of this treasure, delicate and fragile to behold." The same bold *M* adorned the page.

"Who is *M*, or should I not ask?" queried Vivian.

"I don't know," was all Angelique could say. First the huge bouquet, and now the single pale rose..."

"Well, whoever sent this," Vivian said interrupting Angelique's thoughts, "is a romantic. I hope he's also tall, dark, handsome and unattached for your sake."

Turning toward the den, Angelique gestured with her outstretched hand for Vivian to go into that room. "Oh my God!" was all Vivian could say as she gazed wide-eyed at the arrangement that entirely covered the surface of Angelique's cherry wood secretary in the corner. With a questioning stare Vivian searched her friend's face.

"I have no idea who *M* is, so don't ask. I just hope it's not some crazy whose next action is to stalk me," Angelique stated rather dryly.

"Let me see the card," Vivian said. "Did you see this arrow at the bottom of the card? There's more written on the reverse side." With their heads together the two read the message together. "My identity is not a secret, and I mean you no harm. Please accept this small token of my friendship. We were friends once."

"Who is this, Angel? Think! He's either crazy about you, or just plain crazy!"

The pleasure of the picnic in the park was tainted. The food was scrumptious and plentiful, and a light breeze kept the tree boughs bobbing in the wind, but Angelique's thoughts kept drifting back to the recent startling events. Who was responsible for the flowers and the cryptic notes? Having made the decision to increase the security system already in place in her home, Angelique allowed the hint of a smile to play around the edges of her luscious lips.

Chapter Eleven

Vivian's Lament

"Angel, I'm so confused now about my feelings for Jamal." Vivian's voice had taken on a pensive tone. The words seemed to erupt from an unbidden well deep inside her spirit. There was pain and hurt brimming in her eyes from the tears held at bay.

"Angel...Angel!" Vivian cried in frustration. "You haven't heard a word I've said, have you?" Looking sheepish, Angel looked down before she answered.

"I'm sorry...no I haven't," Angel offered, looking penitent at her friend who always had a ready ear for her. "It must be about Jamal, though, because I haven't seen you this detached in ages."

"It shows, huh?" Vivian asked rhetorically. "Well, I could never fool you for long," Vivian mused forlornly. "I miss him. For two years now we've been each other's best friend and confidant, but now that the issue of marriage has popped up, Jamal walks around like he has something to hide. We just can't get together anymore without one of us snapping at the other."

Angelique knew how hard it was for Vivian to admit that her relationship with Jamal was in trouble, so she reclined on the blanket they had spread under a dogwood tree, heavy with blooms, and said not a word. Now was the true test of her friendship with Vivian. It would have been easy for her to begin berating Jamal, but Angelique sensed her friend needed to voice her pain and be heard. As Vivian faced the scary possibility of her life without Jamal, Angelique reflected on the emptiness she too felt.

As the afternoon turned to early evening, Vivian had gone through a catharsis. At the same time, a plan had been slowly forming in Angelique's head. She would devise a way to make Jamal realize how much he wouldn't want to be without Vivian. Somehow, Angelique could always offer insightful advice for her friend, but could never seem to have that same insight into her own relationships. Slowly unfolding her legs from the lotus position she had assumed, Angelique announced she had better things to do than listen to a sob story.

"Listen," Angel spoke sternly, shaking a perfectly polished fingernail at Vivian, "it's not time to lay down and claim defeat; it's time for action, and I've got just the plan. Let's get out of here and I'll tell you all about it on the way back." Vivian let a slow smile transform her troubled expression as she shook her head, resplendent with heavy curls, in amazement. She was willing to allow the fleeting possibility that Angelique just might be able to accomplish the impossible. For the first time all day, Vivian permitted herself to relax. She had been a bundle of nervous energy waiting to implode earlier. For now she would grab the brass ring of hope Angel proffered, and ride on a current of positive energy.

The notoriety from her published best sellers brought Angelique many attractive offers from publishing houses and magazine companies across the nation. One such lucrative offer, from D.C. Press, an independently owned Black publishing company, proved to be a godsend. Angelique had always identified with the African American culture in the United States, since her heritage was Polynesian, French Moroccan and Black. As a renowned writer and woman of color she had been impressed by the featured articles in *Male/Female*, one of the company's star publications, and took pride in being asked to do freelance. She would receive recognition for her work and could become a featured writer in every issue if she so chose. For now Angelique was happy to do the freelance articles.

Flipping through her mail, Angel was particularly enthused with a letter and invitation that had come in the mail today from its editor. A two-day conference and black-tie affair were being held in three weeks in Washington, D.C. "My plan is coming together sooner than I had anticipated," Angel realized. The consulting firm Vivian presided over was intimately linked with the magazine Angel wrote for. The black-tie affair was just the event to get Vivian's and Jamal's relationship back on track. As much as she was sure Jamal wanted his freedom, she couldn't believe he would stand still and let someone walk off with his woman. Not if she could help it. A provocative smile slowly spread across Angelique's lovely face as she bent her head in contemplation.

~

Vaguely Angelique heard the soft din of the doorbell. She had come to accept this daily 2:00 ritual. It had been a week. Sighing softly she roused herself from her matchmaking plans. Just having luxuriated in a jasmine scented bubble bath, Angelique was wearing silk pajamas with a matching floor length robe. Her hair had been tied up with a ribbon for her bath, and shiny tendrils had escaped, making their way down her delicate cheek. Without hesitation Angel pulled open her front door, expecting her usual deliveryman with one pale rose. Totally unprepared for this visitor, she backed away in fright, with an anguished shriek muffled in her throat.

Clad in a short-sleeved cream-colored vee neck polo shirt and denim jeans that fit his rugged contours, Paul Monroe stood, radiating sensuality and sexuality. The curly hairs on his chest peeked through the opening of the shirt and his long, lean muscular thighs were prominent. Angelique also took in the bulging biceps that reminded her of a weightlifter. Looking chaste and sensuous at the same time, Paul stepped back slightly, an apology on his lips.

"Angel, I didn't mean to frighten you," he began, "but I thought it was time we talked." From behind his back he extended his hand which held a perfect pale peach rose.

"You!" Angel sputtered. "It was you who was sending these flowers?" A look of incredulity filled Angelique's expression. It seemed as if an eternity passed before Paul finally broke the spell.

"May I come in?" Paul managed to say while his eyes were locked on Angelique's. The timber of his voice had deepened noticeably; it was husky and full of longing. The air was heavy with desire, and it took Angelique some moments to gather herself. She was certain Paul could hear the thud of her heartbeat as he narrowed the distance between them. Stepping slightly aside she allowed him to enter, steeling herself to the emerging wild emotions bringing her blood to a fevered pitch.

Gesturing for him to follow her into her cozy den, Angelique turned sharply. She had slipped her armor back on as she gazed at him coolly from beneath her lush curly lashes.

"Why have you come, and why did you find it necessary to ply me with flowers?"

"You didn't like them?" he asked, ignoring the hostility in her voice.

"Yes, they were beautiful..."

"But not as beautiful as you," Paul replied before Angelique could finish her sentence. "Angel, I was serious when I said I had been looking for you. After you disappeared, I nearly went out of my mind. Later, I found you had been safely returned, but I couldn't get near your mother or Jack to ask about you. My phone calls were not returned either."

"Tell me," Angel began with ice in her voice, "how much were you paid to pretend to care for me and set me up?"

In one swift stride Paul was standing directly in front of Angel. He tenderly clasped her hands in his and brought them to his lips, brushing her hands with a tender kiss. Spying a loveseat in the cozy den, and heady with the scent of the previous weeks' drought of blooms, Paul gently guided Angelique to the seat for two. With unmistakable sincerity shinning in his eyes Paul calmly began to recount for Angelique the horror he faced waking in St. Albans

Hospital, blind and disoriented, and with no idea of her whereabouts. They talked for hours until the sun, once high in the sky, was low as a beacon drawing all straggling wayfarers to shore.

A tentative peace was achieved. Angelique decided she would give Paul a chance to prove himself. If he failed, all the sweeter her revenge would be. Besides, what did he have to gain now? Even if she couldn't admit to herself that she reveled in the thought that Paul cared for her, and more importantly, that she still had unresolved feelings for Paul, a calm seemed to seep into her pores at the mere nearness of him. As dusk settled the two destined lovers sat side-by-side, needing to touch but holding back. Time was everything, and the time was not right.

Chapter Twelve

Troubled Waters

Sleeping fitfully, soft whimpering sounds escaped Vivian's slightly parted lips. Even in a troubled sleep she was beautiful. The ivory lace curtains adorning her bedroom window flapped unmercifully in the late evening breeze, but the inert form curled in a fetal position in the center of the queen-sized bed was drenched in sweat. Beads of perspiration dotted her brow and formed a mustache above her top lip. Like marionettes marching in time to a drumbeat, Vivian envisioned herself marching down the aisle of a graceful old gothic church filled with fragrant orchids on her wedding day.

The wedding dress was of cream silk-satin crepe accented by matching hand-sewn pearls on the bodice front. Ivory rosebuds meandered along the waistline and trailed down the slim, slightly puffed long sleeves. Its neckline plummeted modestly to just above the swell of Vivian's ripe full bosom, with a deep vee in the back ending at her waist. Her headdress was of simple baby's breath, intricately entwined in her lustrous wavy hair, which heavily draped her shoulders. Up ahead she could see the proud back of Jamal, standing straight and majestic in his cream-colored tuxedo and cummerbund.

The jubilant smile on her face matched those of the well-wishers filling the pews, only to shatter as each person she passed turned toward her with a face of stone. The guests' heads loomed before her like concrete blocks, their frozen smiles turned to grimacing horrors. As she looked down at the bouquet she clasped in her hands, the petals became wriggling worms. Vivian thrust them from herself and fled in fright as the onlookers boisterously laughed. Bolting upright, Vivian was awakened by the sounds of her own mewling screams echoing in her head, as she did each night the monstrous dream stole into her subconscious.

Across town Angelique lay under a light coverlet, reflecting on the incredible feelings that surged through her body as she savored the memory of being in Paul's arms again. She had still wanted to hate him with all her might, but a part of her wanted to believe Paul had been an unsuspecting participant in her kidnapping. Snuggling against her pillow, Angelique had been mesmerized by the touch of his hands as his held hers captive just hours ago. Her senses had become drugged as she inhaled his once forgotten yet familiar fresh scent of sandalwood, mingled with his natural essence.

Angelique had tried to appear impervious to the nearness of Paul as they sat with thighs faintly brushing on the plush loveseat in her den. She was sure he could hear the distinct hammering of her heart as her pulse throbbed in her ears. Angelique could still feel the tingle from the brush of Paul's lips as he bent low to plant a kiss on her cheek in parting. She had been startled at his quick movement, and the turn of her cheek brought Paul's sensuous, soft, full lips to her own. The air was charged with the heat that passed between them.

Not wanting to break the bond, Paul cradled Angelique's head in his hand as he gently brought her to him. A storm of emotions was raging within Paul as he caressed her lips with his. A burning hunger for Angelique's sweet lips took control of him. He deepened the kiss and Angelique responded, allowing him to enfold her in his arms. The pressure of her full breasts against Paul's chest nearly drove him wild with desire, but he held back. Paul was determined to regain Angelique's trust. He would be patient.

~

The date of the conference and black-tie affair were mere days away now. Vivian was also invited due to her affiliation with the publishing house. This was an affair Angelique knew Vivian would be attending because not to would mean instant death in her profession. Angelique helped Vivian choose the most flattering business suit for the conference, and made sure they both had been pampered and properly groomed from the crown of their heads to the tips of their toes. Both women circulated at the conference, and from the enviable looks they both received from the assorted women, compared to the admiring gazes of the eligible and prestigious men, Angelique was sure Jamal would rethink his desire for freedom before this day had come to an end. The two-day conference ended Saturday afternoon at 3:00, giving each participant a few hours to refresh and return for the black-tie affair at 7:00 p.m.

The Embassy Hotel in Northwest Washington, D.C. had been chosen as the site of the affair. The hotel catered to the wealthy, and no expense had been spared to accommodate the slightest whim or desire of the coddled rich. The surroundings were sumptuous in their opulent attention to detail. Angelique and Vivian retired to Angel's home following the conference to rest before the evening affair. Having relaxed her wariness of Paul, Angel had asked him to accompany her to the affair. Jamal was escorting Vivian as planned, and Angelique was sure that if the attention Vivian had received at the conference was an indication of Vivian's desirability, Jamal would have to prove himself worthy of her this night.

As one might have expected, Vivian received appreciative glances and some very welcome conversation from a number of the male attendees during the affair. True to form, Jamal seemed to experience a dazzling revelation when he saw with his own eyes the covetous looks bestowed on Vivian from the impeccably dressed, highly educated and successful businessmen. He was quite solicitous of Vivian, as if he suddenly realized what a jewel he had in his possession. Time would tell if this new enlightenment would help solidify he and Vivian's relationship, or if this was merely male *machismo* at play.

"That's the funniest story I've ever heard," Angelique replied as she threw her head back to thoroughly enjoy her laugh. She had been talking with Edward Morgan, the handsome and very eligible bachelor and editor of a prominent New York based magazine. He and

Angelique had dated briefly after her divorce from Josh, but the relationship had come too soon after her emotional upheaval. Angelique had not been ready. Edward was obviously still interested and had seized this opportunity to possibly rekindle a flame. Out of the corner of her eye Angelique noticed Paul talking very animatedly to a stunningly beautiful woman. Paul's back was to her, so he hadn't witnessed the look that instantly appeared across her face. But Edward had.

"Angelique, is something the matter?" came the deep baritone voice, piercing her thoughts and bringing her back to the present. "You haven't heard a word I was saying."

"What?" Angel softly uttered, looking perplexed. "Oh...I'm sorry Edward. I don't know what happened." But she did, and so did Edward.

"Your escort," Edward began, "Is it serious?"

"You mean Paul?" Angel managed to whisper, "No," she replied in a firmer voice now. "He's an old friend I knew years ago. The woman with him startled me. She reminded me, for an instant, of a dear friend I lost," she lied. Angelique had no intention of letting Edward, or anyone else for that matter, know how she felt about Paul Monroe. But how did she really feel? The reality of her actions surprised her.

Angel had been having a wonderful time this evening, trading stories with longtime friends, and basking in the attention she had discreetly received by an occasional former interest, and that of the various hopefuls. She hadn't behaved in a manner disrespectful to Paul who had brought her to the affair either. They had dined, talked and danced with one another during the evening, and by mutual consent, began to mingle with the other guests. But now Angel found herself feeling jealous of the beautiful woman who seemed to hold Paul's attention captive.

Silently Angelique berated herself..."Why do I care who Paul talks to? He means nothing to me!" But even as she thought these words Angel knew on another level that she was lying to herself, just as she had lied to Edward moments earlier. Peering up at Edward Morgan through thick black lashes that curled provocatively, Angelique drew in a startled breath. Right in front of her eyes here stood a tall, very handsome man who obviously still very much cared for her. It was obvious in his solicitous manner, and the way he hung onto her every word. It was as if he wanted to drink in Angelique's very essence.

The remainder of the evening passed as a blur to Angelique. She smiled, laughed and responded correctly at the appropriate times in her effort to mingle successfully. Her thoughts, however, were centered on the exotic looking woman who, she discovered, had been a part of Paul's past, and who seemed to have captured his full attention. Vivian more than once caught the faraway look in Angelique's eyes.

"Hey, little Nubian princess," she cajoled, "it looks like you've just slain one mighty warrior, namely Edward Morgan, with your devastating attributes. Why are you zoning out?"

"Huh?" Angelique managed to stammer out, looking as if she had lost something, but not sure what.

"Snap out of it," Vivian whispered demurely, with a beguiling bright smile, "everyone is watching you; you've been acting peculiar for the past hour."

Noting the veiled distress in her friend's eyes, Angelique forcefully brought herself out of her reverie. Smiling at her friend and confidant, she quietly responded, "I've been on a surprising journey. I'll have to tell you about it when I've sorted it out myself." Catching the glint in Angelique's eye, Vivian thoughtfully postponed pursuing the myriad of questions on the tip of her tongue. Later, when they arrived back at Angelique's home would be time enough. "Besides," Vivian thought to herself, "I'm going to concentrate on not

concentrating so hard on Jamal. I like how this evening is turning out."
Just as Vivian turned away from Angelique, there stood Jamal,
beaming with pride, and a look of desire mingled with impatience.

"It looks like I've hit a home run with that man," Vivian
thought to herself with a knowing smile; "he looks as if he can't wait
to get me alone. But I have news for him. After this evening this man
will have to prove himself to me all over again. Then I'll welcome
him with open arms." Masking these thoughts behind a provocative
smile, Vivian looped her arm through Jamal's, intent on letting him
drink in her heady perfume. It was time for him to be left wanting for
a change. Then his victory, winning back Vivian, would be all the
sweeter.

Chapter Thirteen

Loose Ends

Edward proved himself to be a man who would go after what he wanted with no restrictions. During the past few weeks following the black-tie affair he had managed to lure Angelique away from her hectic schedule to go horseback riding and parasailing. And now he had packed a picnic basket with enough tempting delights to assault her senses and force her to accept his well-planned rendezvous. Angelique visibly relaxed as she took in the breath-taking beauty of the landscape as the car slowly meandered along route 66, on through Manassas, Virginia. With Edward at the wheel of his four-wheel drive Lincoln Corsair, Angelique settled back to drink-in the beauty of the verdant Blue Ridge Mountain area. Risking a glance at her silent companion, Angel decided to engage Edward in conversation. He had been more than a little quiet during this trip, and that was out of character for him.

"I know this is an old cliché," Angel began, "but a penny for your thoughts."

Somewhat startled, Edward gave Angel an appreciative glance before replying. "This may sound ironic," he began, "but I was thinking about you, and what it will take to convince you that a relationship with me could be just what we both need." Angelique wasn't quite prepared for Edward's frank honesty. And she wasn't prepared to commit herself to anyone or anything save her novels at present. But she knew she couldn't throw Edward away again. There might be some truth in what he just said.

"You do believe in coming straight to the point, don't you," Angel replied. "But you can't be certain I'm what you need. Why don't we both relax, enjoy each other other's company and see how far we want to take this."

"That's fair enough," Edward replied with a smile, "although with you I never can be sure which way you'll turn, and I don't want to lose you like I did the last time."

Angel started to protest, but Edward shushed her saying, "It's okay, I know I came on too strong before, but Angel, I can't seem to get you out of my system." With a deep sigh he continued, "But unlike last time, I have no timetable, no do or die agenda. If we click that's great, we'll both be happier. If not, we'll continue - and I put emphasis on continue - to be friends. I want a woman in my life who wants me for who I am, not what I can do for her. I'm attracted to you, Angel, because you don't really need anyone. You would want to be with me, I feel, because you would simply want me to be a part of your life. You're established, though I would want you anyway."

"What am I saying...I'm crazy about you woman!" Pulling off to the side of the road Edward brought his car to a stop, and reached for Angel saying, "I'm going to just shut my mouth." And with that he pulled her into his strong embrace. His lips explored her face tenderly, planting butterfly kisses from the tip of her nose to the hollow of her throat. Melding his lips to hers, he unleashed a burning passion within Angel. Savoring the kiss for what seemed an eternity, Edward finally released Angelique.

The innocent kiss had deepened for both of them, bringing a dilemma onto Angelique's shoulders. Edward was a man from her recent past who had never hurt her, someone who consistently offered her warmth and affection. She was drawn to him. On the other hand, there was Paul, the enigma from her youth, who had dropped back into her life unexpectedly. Angelique had strong feelings for him too. "How can I care deeply for two men at the same time?" she wondered.

"I'm sorry," she heard Edward say. "Maybe I shouldn't have said what I did," Edward began, "and about that kiss..." But before he could finish Angelique shushed him with a finger to his soft, full lips.

"Don't apologize," she said with a smile. "We both knew that was coming; we both enjoyed it." Angel sliced through the tension in the air with her next comment, "Now let's see how fast you can get us to that supposedly fabulous picnic site. I'm ravenous!" Shifting back into the driver's seat with a smile on his lips, Edward was much more relaxed than before. Gone was the storm cloud that had been brewing between his bunched eyebrows. Hope was coursing through Edward's bloodstream, and the surge of adrenalin made him feel invincible. If he had his way, Angelique Sterling would be Mrs. Edward Morgan before the coming year was out.

The unplanned escape for Angelique this past weekend had been enjoyable, but made her realize, all the more, that the feelings she had for Paul were very real. "I must be losing my mind," Angelique thought. "I can't be falling for Paul all over again. He's hardly spent any time with me since the black-tie affair, whereas Edward has made it plain he wants a serious relationship." This was very true. But Paul hadn't neglected to call Angel or send the pale peach colored rose that became his signature. More importantly, though, Angelique couldn't resist following up on the little information she had been able to gather on the woman who seemed to dazzle Paul the evening he escorted Angelique to the black-tie affair.

Angelique had learned that the woman's name was Monique Dubois, and that they had known each other some years before. The extent of the friendship was something Angel had not been able to determine. "She's an old friend from years ago," was all Paul volunteered when Angel asked about his *friend*. With Paul giving so little information, Angelique was convinced he was deliberately keeping something from her. The Paul Angelique remembered was usually so open, so candid in his conversations, that his reluctance to say more about Monique piqued Angelique's curiosity.

With marked determination Angelique swiftly placed a call to Captain Maxwell F. Franklin assigned to the special task force of the 125th police district in Washington, D.C. Over the years and through Angelique's early nightmarish kidnapping, the two had become fast friends. Max, as everyone called him, laughingly joked that the *F* stood for fierce. There was never a truer statement. His physical appearance as short and stocky with a slow, winsome smile and slightly receding hairline belied the intensity and ruthlessness with which he pursued each lead to solve the many unsolvable cases that ultimately wound up on his desk.

When Angel's call came through this morning to Capt. Franklin, he hesitated just a moment. Although he had been smitten years ago by Angelique, his *little one*, as he affectionately thought of her, he had to compose himself before taking her call. For Angelique to call him at work meant one thing. She had a problem.

"Hello Max," Angelique purred into the mouthpiece. "I'm glad you could take my call so quickly, but now I'm feeling a little foolish," Angelique admitted with a little nervous laugh.

"This is a new twist," Max thought aloud.

"What did you say?" Angelique intoned.

"Nothing. Listen, I'm all ears; what is it you need?"

Feeling a bit miffed that Max perceived her call as one of wanting something, Angelique began to retract her request. "I don't mean to always call you when I'm in need. I'll let you go and..."

"Nonsense!" bellowed Max. "We've known each other too long. You know I enjoy hearing from you, and I didn't mean to offend you. Whatever I have, you know you've got it!"

Angelique realized Max was placating her, but she really wanted to put an end to the mystery surrounding Monique.

"Can you meet me downtown for lunch one day this week?" she quietly asked.

"For you, anytime, but let's make it tomorrow at 12:30. I have business I'm wrapping up near Connecticut Avenue. We can lunch at Gary's near Dupont Circle and you can fill me in on everything."

"It's a date," Angelique heard herself say, and quickly rang off. She had hoped the mention of lunch would tempt Franklin into agreeing to meet with her today, but since she had said one day this week she would have to wait.

"One more day, one more day," she found herself repeating. "So close..." In the meantime Angelique had a deadline to meet with her publisher, and her thoughts were not flowing as freely as they usually did. She was engrossed in developing the plot surrounding her main character as always, but her personal affairs were distracting her. The concentration she needed to develop her plot was missing. Trying to convince herself that she was gathering ideas to push forward on another storyline did not work. She'd be fooling no one but herself.

At this same time across town sat three other individuals contemplating their personal lives: Paul was still in love with Angelique, but seeing Monique had stirred up memories of the two of them before there was an Angelique; Jamal was certain he was ready to take the plunge and ask for Vivian's hand in marriage. But who was the tall, dark *warrior* escorting his woman home the other evening? It was a full fifteen minutes he had waited outside Vivian's complex that night after seeing her and the strange man enter her home. The man had not left, and Jamal stalked off, seething with disgust at himself for spying on Viv, and anger at her for believing she would be true to him. Hadn't he learned the hard way that you can't trust any woman, not even a *good* one?

And alone sat Vivian. She and Ted had slaved into the wee hours working on the details for a fundraiser. Not wanting to miss a call from Jamal, she had convinced Ted, her assistant, to come to her place and hammer out the last-minute details. She was a known workaholic and didn't want to be always caught in the office. Now Jamal wasn't returning her calls. What had happened to all that *steam and passion* that had slowly built up between them from the night of the black-tie affair? Was this a game? Vivian was miserable and didn't know who or what to blame. When things are going right it feels so good to be riding high. And when bad things happen you think, and hope, it won't/can't get any worse. It usually does.

~

With deft strokes Angelique applied the last few touches to her makeup. A light brush of blush across her cheeks, a shimmer of pale peach shadow on her eyelids and matching lip gloss completed the effect. She was keyed up at the prospect of finally resolving the mystery of who Monique Dubois was and what she meant to Paul. "Damn!" Angel said aloud as she stepped outside. The drizzle that started a few moments ago had turned into a downpour. Wrapping her gray London Fog around her lithe form, Angel snatched a matching umbrella from the stand near the door and dashed quickly to her car.

Traffic was light and Angelique was making good time. Suddenly there was a loud fwuump!! Bump! Bump! Without getting out of her car, Angel knew she had a flat tire. "Of all times for this to happen!" she muttered. Reaching for her purse for her cell phone she realized, too late, it wasn't there. The phone she had purchased for just such emergencies now sat nestled with her driving gloves and wallet in her foyer. Exasperated, Angel pulled off to the shoulder of the road with her head slumped on the steering wheel. The sudden blaring sound and flashing lights startled her. A sigh of relief escaped her lips as the police cruiser eased up behind her mahogany metallic colored Porsche. The respite was momentary; suddenly Angel realized her driver's license sat with her purse back at home!

At this same time a turbulent conversation was taking place across town. "Well, hello," Vivian replied smoothly to Jamal's curt, "Leonard here," on answering his phone.

"You've been on my mind," Vivian softly stated, "and I was worried about you."

The irritation never left his voice as Jamal caustically replied, "Really? I can't imagine why. You know I travel frequently in my line of work." Not sure where this hostility, just simmering beneath the surface stemmed from, Vivian ignored the lack of warmth and affection she longed to hear in Jamal's tone and plodded on.

"Baby, I thought it would be nice to spend some quiet time together this evening, and..."

"Impossible," he shot back without giving Viv a chance to finish. "My schedule won't permit the luxury. And frankly, I haven't the time to waste."

As the words slipped from between his lips Jamal loathed the very sound of his voice to his own ears. He could feel the hurt well up inside the woman he loved, and knew he had administered a stinging emotional blow, when he heard her sudden intake of breath. He could almost see Vivian blinking rapidly as she often did when confused or frustrated. At that moment Jamal wanted to comfort her, but the image of the *other man* loomed before him.

Funny how a week ago he would not have pictured the two of them apart, with him hurtling scorching barbs at his precious baby. But then a week ago he had no thought of Vivian betraying him with another man. Jamal could still see the image of Vivian and the tall stranger furtively hurrying into her townhouse. It was just three days ago, but it seemed as if an eternity had passed. "Well that's that," he thought to himself. To Vivian he simply replied, "I've got to go. I'll be seeing you around." And with that the line went dead.

Vivian stared at the phone as if it was a foreign object. "I'll be seeing you around?" she screamed. Grief stricken, the tears that had welled up in her eyes gushed forth as sobs racked her body. She was dumbfounded at this drastic reversal from Jamal. Only last week he had cradled her in his arms, proclaiming her his woman, holding her securely in his loving arms. After several long moments Vivian straightened up. "Well, if that's the way he wants it, fine."

"I'm sorry miss, I need to see your driver's license and registration. If you can't produce them, I'll have to give you a ticket for operating a motor vehicle without a valid driver's license." This was the second request by the young officer, who was becoming impatient with Angelique.

"But if you would just call Capt. Franklin...I'm on my way to meet him."

"Miss, I can't do that. I can get you some assistance for that flat tire, but I will have to give you a ticket. You will be expected to appear in court."

Tears that had pooled in the corners of Angelique's eyes, held captive by sheer will power, began their descent down her creamy, smooth cheek. A torrent was unleashed that seemed to have no end. All the pent-up anxiety and frustration Angel had kept bottled up now poured forth, to the chagrin of the young officer, who was as perplexed as Angelique was distraught.

With a flat tire and ticket, Angel hailed a taxi in the drizzling rain. She decided to return home for her purse and phone and take the same taxi straight to the restaurant. Under no circumstances would she risk being late for her meeting with Max. Too much was at stake. "I can always call roadside assistance from the restaurant to have my flat fixed," she mused. Plus, she was in no state to drive.

The polished, chic, woman in control had vanished, and in her place stood a frazzled, stressed-out Angelique; a shell of her former self. Quite forlornly she requested to be taken to Capt. Franklin's table by the headwaiter at Gary's restaurant, a midtown restaurant on M Street in D.C. At the sight of her, Maxwell Franklin jumped to his feet, alarmed at the obvious change in Angel's demeanor. She had not meant to cry and appear weak, but without warning the trembling that started at the corner of her eyes ushered in a torrent of tears.

Quietly dabbing at the spill with a handful of tissues, Angel related the details of her encounter with the police officer and the past events that culminated in tears and her feelings of despair. Maxwell attempted to calm her as he would a lost child, talking calmly and soothingly, all the while sifting fact from fiction to discover the truth behind Angelique's apparent distress.

"A brandy for the lady, please," Maxwell requested as the waiter nervously approached, not sure if he should interrupt the diners. Their shoulders were hunched so as not to let a bit of conversation stray to any other tables.

"Yes sir, and for you?"

"A caffe mocha for me," Maxwell replied to the waiter, and to Angel, "I'm still officially on duty. Otherwise I'd enjoy a brandy too."

After a delicious luncheon on broiled swordfish with an exquisite side salad that tantalized her taste buds, Angelique reveled in the comfortable atmosphere of Gary's restaurant. It was clearly dominantly male with its trappings of wall hangings and Naugahyde. Yet strength and power were not strangers to Angelique. It was her inner strength that had kept Angel on her feet all these years when others less formidable would have crumpled. She had survived so many tragic situations that Franklin was at first shaken by Angel's countenance.

"So pretty lady, exactly what do you want me to uncover?"

The sound of Maxwell's deep bass brought Angelique back to the main reason for this afternoon luncheon. With little fanfare and much humility Angelique lost no time in extracting a promise from her dear friend to lend his assistance. With the information she was sure to obtain, Angelique brightened up considerably, allowing the confident woman that she was to take hold of the reins. With a sigh Maxwell Franklin wondered what it would have felt like to have Angelique enamored of him. But such thoughts were a digression in nonsense, and he had the good sense to accept the sisterly love she offered.

"Max, you and I have been friends for a long time, but I don't want to impose on our friendship."

"Nonsense," cried Captain Franklin. "What are friends for if they can't help one another? Now, what can I do to remove that worried look from your face?"

Max was a good and kind man, but Angel had never had a romantic thought for him. Even though she felt he secretly cared for her, more than as a friend, she felt compelled to ask for his help.

"I need some information on someone. A woman named Monique Dubois. Let me tell you why."

Angel revealed that Paul Monroe was someone from her past, and that she had suddenly encountered him again after many years. Since she had met him shortly before her abduction, she wouldn't consider a relationship with Paul until she had information about his background. Angel knew Max could discreetly make inquiries without drawing unnecessary attention to himself or to her. She also needed to know the tie between Monique and Paul.

Max tried hard to keep the hurt from his eyes and voice as he began to ask Angel a few necessary questions. He had secretly hoped he would someday be able to let Angel know of his feelings for her. Now a man from her past thwarted him. After jotting down the necessary names and other vital facts in his notebook, Max snapped it shut with too much force. Noting Angel's startled look he laughed quickly to cover his frustration.

Pretending to be in a good mood he began, "Now that we've gotten that business out of the way, what say you and I take a short drive? You look like you need a friend?" With that said, Max signaled the waiter for the check. He refused to let Angel pay. Gently he held her elbow and escorted her from the restaurant to his unmarked car.

"Since you don't have your car and you still have a flat tire, I'll drive you home and have someone change the tire and bring your car to you this afternoon, if that's okay with you."

"Yes, thank you so much," Angel replied, handing over her car keys to Max as she slid onto the seat of his car.

"I feel so foolish though."

"Don't give it a second thought. It's no trouble at all." With that said the pair exited the parking lot to salvage what was left of the afternoon. The light rainfall that had softly begun to fall shortly after Angelique entered the restaurant had stopped. Now that the sun had reappeared Angel's spirits were renewed. Perhaps she would have her questions answered favorably and have a chance at the solace she so desperately sought.

Chapter Fourteen

Memory Lane

Back in the security of her home Angelique breathed a sigh of relief. Her behavior today had been so uncharacteristic of her. Could she really allow Paul Monroe to completely unhinge her? "No, I won't," Angelique asserted to the four walls. "I just need to fill in the missing pieces to the puzzle. Once I've done that I can move on with my life."

Gathering her inner reserve, Angelique decided to seize what was left of this day to reflect on where her travails had taken her. Lying across her four-poster bed listening to the soft drizzle of rain on her windowpanes as a backdrop to the jazz CD she had slipped into her disc player, Angelique fell into a deep sleep. She awakened in her subconscious to the summer of her eighteenth birthday. How hot and sticky was this day, alike yet somehow different from the others she had experienced on the island. Vaguely Angelique sensed an almost feral quality to the air.

After being on the island for the better part of a year Angelique had formed an odd attachment to Damien. She now playfully teased him outright and looked forward to their evening ritual. They now dined together with Angelique attempting to covertly glean any tidbit of information about her benevolent protector. Only once had Damien let slip mention of Mt. Orohena, the highest mountain in the Society Islands, which Angelique had heard her mother mention. Damien recovered quickly, hoping Angelique hadn't been paying too close attention to his musings. Glancing furtively at Angelique, Damien tried to assess whether she had registered his comment.

Angelique, a master at not revealing her true feelings, feigned disinterest, all the while devouring the large salad set before her. She hadn't missed the suddenly sharp intake of breath from Damien. Her poker face belied little, and Damien felt his revelation was missed. Slowly he exhaled and the tension, visible in his eyes, evaporated.

Suddenly he smiled at her very tenderly behind his mask, as with the pride of a father toward his child. In many ways he was the father figure Angelique had grown up without. A wave of sorrow suddenly enveloped Angelique. She would not miss the island and the forced separation from her mother, but she would miss Damien. It was as if she had already begun a period of mourning for him - for no apparent reason - as she sat absorbing the intensity of his eyes, the way the bright noon day sun had bronzed his skin to a ripe warm cinnamon, and his enigmatic smile.

Letting her feet sink into the lush carpet of grass beneath her feet, Angelique slowly moved to capture a bloom for her hair, for Damien's pleasure, from the myriad of lilies abundant on the island. As she turned to face Damien with a sweet smile tugging on the corners of her lips, she became horrified, seeing yet not quite comprehending the spurt of bright red blood issuing from his right shoulder. She had until just now believed the camp to be impenetrable. Without a sound the encampment had been silently surrounded, and what appeared to be guerilla invaders engulfed Damien's stronghold.

Without hesitation Angelique bolted the three feet to Damien's side, tearing a strip of cloth from her clothing to staunch the blood flow. Surprised by her sudden movement, one of the invaders raised his gun to shoot. "Fool!" shouted another gunman, all the while knocking the poised rifle tip to the ground. "We have come for her!" The shouted snatches of conversation, in French, left Angelique feeling clammy in the pit of her stomach. It had been many years since she had conversed in her native tongue, but she had not altogether forgotten it. From the bits of erupted dialogue from the apparent leader, she was not to be harmed.

Damien, who had protected and sheltered her from all harm thus far on the island, was roughly seized. His hands were tied behind his back and he was jerked cruelly to a kneeling position on the ground. Damien locked eyes with Angel and whispered, "It will be alright; be brave for me." Fearing his immediate execution, Angelique snatched free from a towering gunman and began pleading in her native tongue: "Non, s'il vous plez! You must not harm him! He is good! He has been kind! Take whatever you wish, but do not harm him!" Baffled at Angel's outburst, but with strict orders, the gunman hesitated momentarily. This was all the time Damien needed to strike at the gunman. Rising to a semi-standing position Damien lowered his head and butted the gunman, knocking the ruffian off his feet. Mayhem broke out all over. Shots were fired. The women began screaming and crying, fearful of the weapons trained on them.

In the ensuing pandemonium Damien seemed to have disappeared. Angel was unceremoniously grabbed and led through the jungle growth at gunpoint, destination unknown. She had had to walk several miles through thick underbrush that scratched and tore at her skin. Her feet became blistered when holes wore in her sandals, and one of the men was forced to carry her, slung over his shoulder, the rest of the journey. At the end of the seemingly endless trek Angelique and the band of rescuers came to a clearing on the far side of the island. There a helicopter awaited them. Gesturing for her to board the chopper, the gunman made it plain by his closed and angry countenance that he would not reveal Damien's outcome, if he even knew. No question would be answered. This man had obviously come on a specific mission, and now his part was finished.

With apprehension Angelique boarded the chopper, taking the proffered waterskin to slake her thirst. After buckling the seatbelt and taking a few sips of the clear liquid Angelique apparently fell into a drug induced sleep. She awoke in Miami in a small airfield, drifted back to sleep, then found herself onboard an equally small, chartered plane. Who was responsible for this? She was wearing a fresh change of clothes and her blistered feet had been tenderly dressed. Everything about the flight was a blur.

When had she changed over from the helicopter to the plane? When had she changed her clothes? What happened to Damien? Was he alive? Whoever freed her from her island prison made sure her water had been spiked so her senses would be dulled. This may have been done as a kindness for the long journey ahead of her. However, none of her questions had been answered then, and they still remained a mystery to this day.

Chapter Fifteen

Present Tense

An incessant thrumming began to form in the back of Angel's head. Somewhere far off she could faintly hear a small voice calling her name. There was urgency in the tone, but Angel was reluctant to respond. She was nestled in the cocoon of sleep. But the sound grew louder, and against her will Angel's eyes opened, taking in her surroundings. She was in her bedroom, and not in Miami. She had not recently been separated from Damien. The cacophony of knocking and doorbell ringing pierced her quiet and Angel swung her legs over the side of the bed, trying to further orient herself.

"I'm coming! I'm coming!" she yelled at her front door as she padded silently down the deeply carpeted stairs. With an angry scowl to match her mood, Angel swung open the door to a frenzied looking Vivian.

"What on earth..." was all Angel could say before Viv hurtled herself over the threshold, slumping against the wall with a disoriented, haunted look on her face that made Angel shiver.

"What's happened to you?" Angel demanded. "Are you ill? Has something happened to your parents?" Angel implored, remembering her anguish over her own parents' untimely violent deaths.

"No, nothing like that," Vivian managed to say at length. She didn't seem compelled or able to say more for the time being. Realizing her friend needed to work through a few things, Angel sought to sooth her friend until she could open up and grab for the help Vivian so obviously and desperately needed.

"Come on in and I'll make us both a cup of tea," Angel said, guiding Viv to an overstuffed lounger in her den. Angel had just awakened from a restless sleep in which she had been cast back in time to her capture and final day with Damien, her benefactor. Seeing Vivian so emotionally disheveled was having a definite impact on Angelique. She found she had very little control over her own destiny, but could always seem to marshal the insight and sometimes stamina to hold up a failing friend in crisis. This situation with Vivian had all the markings of a human being in dire need.

The plan was simply and swiftly made. The three-and-a-half-hour trip by car proved to be the most taxing part of the plan but allowed Angelique and Vivian time alone. Vivian needed to sort out her feelings and make some sense out of Jamal's actions. One moment he was ready to commit, the next he was treating Viv like a cast off.

The dying sun found the two troubled women sitting on a glider in the vast back yard of family friends in Hampton, Virginia. The distance from their homes allowed the two friends to put the chaos behind them. Catherine and John Freeman had been close friends of Michelle and Jack and were glad to be able to lend their summer home to Angelique on such short notice. The Freeman's children were grown and living abroad so there wasn't much use for the summer place anymore. John and Catherine now enjoyed their freedom, cavorting around Europe and the Mediterranean in their golden years. They had urged Angel to come down to Hampton after Kimmie's death, but Angel had declined. At the time she felt she would somehow be deserting Kimmie.

With her life whirling out of control and her inability to think clearly, Angelique finally realized that she and Vivian both needed time and space to put some perspective on their situations. Casting a sideways glance at Vivian, Angelique broke the silence.

"Do you want to talk about it now?"

Vivian and Angel had enjoyed a companionable silence, by mutual consent, for the last two hours while riding down to Hampton.

With a sign and a shake of her head, Vivian was more than ready to unburden herself.

"Angel, I don't know what's happened since the black-tie affair. Jamal and I were doing great. I was almost sure he was ready to make a commitment to me. I know I've been working long hours, but I've been working at home most evenings. I've even convinced Ted, my assistant, to work some evenings at my place."

"Hold on, did you say Ted has been working at your place?"

"Yes, he lives near me so instead of working late across town we've been finalizing the details for the upcoming fundraiser from my home office. Wait…you don't think…?"

"I think you just answered your own question. Didn't you say Jamal is very jealous and that trust is a big issue with him?"

"Yes, but I'm not being unfaithful to Jamal. Ted is just a friend and employee of mine."

"That may be so, but if Jamal has seen the two of you together, he wouldn't know that. Didn't you also tell me that Jamal works out at the new health club by your place?"

Hesitantly Vivian replied, "Yes…"

"Then that must be it!" exclaimed Angel. "I'll bet Jamal somehow saw the two of you together and jumped to the wrong conclusion!"

"If what you say is true," exclaimed Viv, "Jamal will never believe me if I say there's nothing going on between me and Ted."

"That's right. He won't believe anything you say," replied Angel. "Let me think on this. If I'm correct about all of this, we'll have to plan carefully."

Angel and Viv realized that Jamal would be suspicious of anything Angel said. After some thought Angel asked, "Is Ted seeing anyone?"

"Well, I'm not sure," replied Viv, "but I think so. A couple of evenings he seemed restless while we worked, so I told him we could knock off early. You know, now that I think about it, Ted did seem in a hurry to leave."

"That's good," replied Angel, "that may mean he has a significant other. Does he have any pictures on his desk?" asked Angel.

"I've never noticed any," Viv replied. "Ted is very private."

"Okay," replied Angel, "Let me think for a moment." After some moments of silence Angel asked, "When is the fundraiser?"

"You know it's two weeks from now," replied Viv. "You helped me arrange the fashion show to be held during the luncheon at Martin's Camelot."

"That's it!" Angel cried, smiling broadly. "Only, let's expand the luncheon to include the board of directors and other stakeholders. That would include me, and of course, Jamal. And suggest your staff bring dates. I'll ask Jamal to accompany me; he wouldn't dare refuse as a fellow board member."

"I can do one better," said Viv. I'll send the board personal invitations for the $500.00 a plate affair. After all, it will be a tax write off. We just need to make sure Ted has a date for the affair."

Chapter Sixteen

Revelations

Capt. Maxwell F. Franklin

Maxwell F. Franklin, clad in blue jeans and a black short-sleeved Tee shirt, sat in his very masculine den, moodily stirring his rare mug of black coffee. The pensive expression on his face belied the beautiful sunny day outside, or the fact that it was Saturday morning, the day Max had looked forward to all week. You wouldn't have known from looking at him that in just one hour he would be headed for an extended getaway to a tropical paradise. But with the information Max had just received, the trip would prove to be no holiday.

At times like this when Max was troubled with some point in an investigation, he would usually retire to his favorite leather recliner, surrounded by row upon row of books in his oak paneled library. Today he sat in a hard straight-back chair behind a massive oak desk, a habit reminiscent of his days many years ago as a private investigator. He had been a P.I. long before joining the police force. It was his uncanny investigative skills, intuitive instinct and a basic understanding of human nature that gave him the edge over many older men in this field. These traits also ultimately propelled him into his career of law enforcement. Because Max usually uncovered damaging facts that irreparably altered so many lives, he gave up this line of work for police work.

"Maybe I'm getting soft," Max had said on many occasions. But the ingredients for scandal he unearthed had taken its' toll on him.

"I've got to feel I can make a difference where it really counts," he mused aloud to no one. "I don't want to be the reason someone gets taken to the cleaners in a divorce court. I need to solve crimes that can help the victims, or their families, put closure on their tragedies."

And thus Maxwell "Max" Franklin threw himself into the mind of the criminal for the police department. Plus, he felt he needed to put some distance between himself and the shady characters who befriended him and with whom he had come to rely on to *get the dirt* for his clients. Max became homicide's best detective, steadily rising in rank ahead of many seasoned officers on the force. In spite of his youth and his torpedo rise in rank, no one begrudged his accomplishment. Max was humble and never forgot to give credit where credit was due.

Now Max found himself in a dilemma. Angel had asked him for information on Paul Monroe and Monique Dubois. In response to her request he had uncovered some very intriguing and powerful information that, in the wrong hands, could ultimately destroy Angelique. In his investigation Max had unwittingly uncovered evidence concerning Angel's abduction that even the FBI had not been able to discover. But then Max had a sixth sense, or ability if you will, at linking seemingly unrelated facts and events. He also had the privilege of several informants only too eager to *spill their guts* to Max in return for his putting in a good word for them. Their cooperation could result in them receiving lighter sentences or shorter imprisonments for their criminal convictions.

With the help of two such informants Max not only had the information Angel requested, but he also now knew the motive for her abduction, and who was ultimately responsible for her horrific ordeal. Following up on a hunch and a tip, he had been able to piece together the whole kidnapping scenario. In disbelief he sat staring at the telephone. The caller was unaware of the importance of the casual remark made about a piece of jewelry that Max knew had gone missing in Angel's abduction case. And now with dread Max suspected dire results from his impending trip. However, he would have to follow this lead at all cost.

"This will destroy my Angel, but I owe her the truth," he cried aloud. "I only hope she will be able to trust her heart again someday."

Max deplaned in the bustling Tahiti International Airport, also known as Faa'a International Airport of French Polynesia, located in the commune of Faa'a on the island of Tahiti. He chose this destination because of the informant's random remarks, and because it was only 5 kilometers, or roughly a little over 3 miles, from Papeete, the capital city of the overseas collectivity. Even though Max had a heavy heart over what he knew he would discover, he planned to enjoy snorkeling and scuba diving in the pristine blue waters. A helicopter tour was also on his list for more than vacation enjoyment. He had hopes of flying near or over the area Angel had been held captive. Hopefully he could make this happen with added financial incentive to the pilot.

The day was warm, 70 degrees, but the humidity was high. Thankfully Max had remembered to bring plenty of mosquito repellent and bottled water. This was not the time to become dehydrated or contract a disease from the bite of vicious, pesky insects plentiful on the island. Not this far from home. After checking into Relais Fenua, a modestly priced resort in Punaauia, Max decided to unwind. The property, set in a tropical garden with a large outdoor swimming pool, was where Max headed immediately after taking a reviving shower. He had chosen well as this was a great location for relaxing. The resort had a TV, private bath and specifically a private terrace where Max could stay in touch through the internet while enjoying breezes from the nearby beach. Plus, it had air conditioning. All this was secondary, however, to the plans Max had to solve the many years old abduction case of Angel, and more specifically, why.

The name Raphael Medici kept popping up in the intel Max had been able to pry from his informant, and in casual conversations with persons with connections to him. He was surprised to uncover

Paul Monroe's connection to Raphael through checking into Jack Montenero's business background. This had been done ever so discreetly using the resources of his police department. He had not turned up anything amiss with Jack, but the dominoes were beginning to fall into place. Max discovered that Paul's mother, Serita, had been briefly in a partnership with Raphael Medici. The gossip Max uncovered depicted Raphael, a person with dubious credentials in the import export business, as shrewd and involved in money laundering some years ago. Also, that Raphael held a misplaced grudge with Jack Montenero behind a late-night meeting that Jack had insisted upon before doing business with him.

Raphael instead had sent Serita, his partner. During Serita's drive from the meeting she encountered Kyle Monroe whom she met on the side of the road following a downpour. Kyle had helped Serita by changing her flat tire outside the city of Puerto Limon in Costa Rica. Raphael not only lost Serita, but also the business deal with Jack since he had refused to show up. Instead of Raphael blaming himself for Serita and Kyle meeting, and eventual romance and marriage, Raphael blamed Jack Montenero. Out of spite Raphael set up his godson, Paul, Serita and Kyle's son, at the ski chalet where Jack, Michelle and Angel vacationed.

With this background information, Max had his work cut out for him. But he vowed to piece the puzzle together before returning stateside. With his month-long vacation Max had ample time, he felt, to make inquiries to uncover the abduction plot. He had seldom taken time off from his job and had more than enough vacation time to unravel the threads of the fine web of mischief.

Chapter Seventeen

The Event of a Lifetime

Once you step into The Camelot, located on the grounds of the historic Evangel Temple in Upper Marlboro, Maryland, you find you've been transported back into another time. You enter into a medieval themed grand ballroom with three ballrooms and seven conference / breakout rooms. Nearly every taste and budget can be accommodated by buffets with chef carving stations. A better venue couldn't have been selected. The award-winning chefs can cater to every kind of diet. Knowing that Viv and a number of her professional associates are vegan and vegetarian played into Angel's choice of venues. She had attended a number of events here and remembered the mouth-watering dishes she had dined on. A satisfied stomach and awe inspiring fashion show would lead to a healthy donation from each of the attendees. This venue would help garner more than enough patrons for this and additional fundraisers to come. The cause was a worthy one. What more could one ask for?

Angel and Viv contacted local entrepreneurs and designers to enlist their help with creating the fashions and selecting the models. As a highlight to the event a special selection of children and teen fashions were also presented. There were also *mommy and daughter* outfits and models, as well as *father and son* outfits and models gracing the runway. Angel and Viv were both presenters during the gala where several scholarships to scholastically worthy upcoming college freshmen would be granted.

One hundred patrons were in attendance and Angel and Viv handled the seating arrangements. After all, this was their chance to help Viv with her dilemma with Jamal. Right on cue Vivian's assistant, Ted, showed up with a lovely young lady on his arm as Jamal sought his seat at his assigned table. There was no question that the two were an item as Ted was very solicitous of his lady. Angel noted the quizzical look on Jamal's face when he saw Ted introduce his lady, Rachel, to Viv. Viv was full of smiles as she gave Ted a platonic hug and a gracious air kiss to his date.

"I hope you will forgive me for working Ted so late into the evening, Rachel," Jamal overheard Viv say to Ted's date, "but we had so little time and so many things to finalize before this event."

"Oh, it was no problem," replied Rachael. "With the two of you working on this side of town, that allowed Ted and I to have more time together in the evenings."

Angel had been discreetly observing the exchange between Rachel and Viv and took note of Jamal, not two feet away, unobtrusively lingering on their every word, while pretending to be absorbed in reading his fund-raising program. Satisfied that Jamal had heard enough, Angel took the opportunity to politely intrude to *request Vivian's help with something* as Ted and Rachel then took their seats at the table where Jamal sat, and introduced themselves.

"Jamal must be feeling really low at this point for mistrusting you," Angel whispered to Vivian, "and it serves him right."

"I made sure I spoke just loud enough for Jamal to hear our exchange," Vivian replied. "And I didn't miss the startled look on his face when Ted showed up beaming with Rachel on his arm to introduce her to me."

"Yes," replied Angel. "I've never seen someone study a program as hard as Jamal was, pretending not to be listening to your conversation. He must feel like a fool for rudely brushing you off. Now he'll have to figure out how to get back in your good graces. Make him sweat!"

"The evening is young yet," said Viv, "but I'm not galloping back into his arms at the first invitation. I've got my pride. Jamal will have to work for my attention. I'm done playing the victim, gulping up the crumbs he scatters for me."

And with that said, the two friends walked off to prepare to announce the recipients of the scholarships before the meal began. Vivian peeked over her shoulder as she left, noticing Jamal deep in thought.

"Good," she mused, "let him wrap his head around the fact that he assumed the worse of me with no facts. Let him stew on that."

Catching her glance, Angel knew exactly what Viv was thinking as the two friends were so close. "Yes," Angel said, "Jamal probably feels like an idiot for mistrusting you and ruining a good relationship. You are the best thing for that man."

At this same time on the far away island of Tahiti Captain Maxwell F. Franklin sat by the pool at his resort nursing a cool drink while waiting for his contact on the island to arrive. Moments later a compact, bronzed man furtively scanned the area before approaching Max.

"La Orana (hello)! You must be Max," said the small man, compared to Max's 5 feet 8 inches. Max shook his hand and gestured to a seat. They made small talk for a bit, then Max got down to the business of his trip. He assured the man that he was not here in any official capacity, had no jurisdiction, and was not looking to have anyone arrested. He just wanted information as a personal investigator for a client. The information was not free and an exchange of money took place. It was worth it. As evening wore on Max had a clearer picture of the events. It was mind blowing how a person could be so petty and harbor such ill will to cause so much harm.

Raphael Medici had been the mastermind behind the whole plot that had unwittingly targeted Angelique instead of Michelle. He had played on Damien's unrequited love and anger with his brother, Jamari, over Michelle, Angel's mother. He had placed Paul at the ski chalet in Montana, on the pretense of a paying job during his semester break, for reconnaissance. Joe, a chalet manager, had been strong armed by Raphael's *associates* for gambling debts he was having trouble paying back. When Paul turned up requesting a job at the chalet Joe's *no* quickly turned to *yes* at the mention of Raphael Medici. Joe knew only too well the long reach of Raphael Medici and the damage he could leave in his wake.

As early evening turned into night the two men's secretive conversation ended. All that was left to discover was whether Jamari had been instrumental in coordinating the kidnapping with Raphael for his own gain? Was Jamari involved in securing the mercenaries who rescued Angel? Did he affect the outcome of the kidnapping after learning it was Angel and not Michelle that had been abducted? Or was he instrumental in gaining Angel's release after learning Damien was involved? It was clear that fatal harm was not intended to Damien who had somehow managed to slip away. But just how did he escape? Who helped him and why? But even more weighty on Max's mind was the information he discovered about Paul Monroe and Monique Dubois before leaving the States.

Even though Angelique proved to be a strong and very resilient young woman, having lived through and surviving so many upheavals and turmoil in her life, Max was sure the *Paul / Monique* news would be devastating. Monique was not simply an ex-girlfriend from Paul's past. She had been his girlfriend at the time Angel and Paul first met and was now the mother of his son. It was true they broke up after Paul had fallen for Angel on the infamous skiing trip, and before either of them knew of the coming child. But there it was. Paul and Monique would forever have a connection through their shared son.

Max learned from reliable sources that Paul and Monique had been childhood friends and had become sweethearts in high school. They attended different colleges but had remained close from their years of friendship. They had once envisioned a life together, but fate now led them in different directions. Monique had not immediately told Paul about the child she was expecting after his head trauma. In truth, she didn't learn about the baby until Paul began going through rehab for his injuries a month later. At the time she did not want to overwhelm him with the news during this fragile time period for him.

When Monique visited Paul in the hospital just after his accident he divulged to her that he had met someone he was emotionally drawn to, had fallen in love with during his semester break. This was the reason Amelia, Paul's nurse, had noticed Monique's discomposure when she left his hospital room. Amelia jealously noticed the strikingly beautiful young woman wiping tears from her eyes. Monique was distressed over Paul's revelation and the end of her future life with him. It mattered little at the time that they vowed to always be honest with each other. The truth hurt. The question remaining was whether Paul's attachment to Monique had deepened during the intervening 10 years that Angel was lost to Paul.

Max mused, "True, Paul and Monique had not married even to this day, but a child would always bind them together." Max sincerely hoped Paul would tell Angel of the son he had with Monique before he laid bare this revelation. He knew that this information coming from him, and not Paul himself would appear that Paul was keeping secrets and make Angel mistrust him even more. Max's confidant had not found any dirt on Paul. He appeared to be an upstanding attorney who could not be bought, worked out routinely at a gym, and gave his time and energy to charitable causes. With this part of Angel's request complete, Max decided to turn in for the night. It had been a tiring day from the flight and he must prepare for tomorrow, to get more intel on Raphael Medici and Damien and Jamari Dupre.

Across the continent the highly successful fund-raising event was coming to a close. Everyone's palate had been satisfied with the many selections of entrees and desserts. Scholarships had been given to five worthy upcoming college students to help during their freshmen year, and the fashion show had been a success hands-down. Several of the entrepreneurial designers had made very lucrative contacts to further their business enterprises. Angel and Viv were congratulating themselves and breathing a sigh of relief that the event had ended with no mishap when Jamal approached the two.

"May I have a word with you, Viv?" Vivian turned to see Jamal behind her with a look on his face she couldn't read.

"I still have a few things to tend to," replied Viv.

"It won't take long," Jamal replied, "and it's important, please."

After noting the sincerity in Jamal's voice and the word *please,* Vivian was now ready to give Jamal a bit of her time. She knew she was due an apology at least and an explanation for his cool reception to her phone calls. But she would not make it easy for him, no matter how much she desired for the two of them to be a committed couple.

Jamal drew Viv into a secluded nook with a bench in the foyer of the hall, took Viv's hands in his and began to lay bare his soul.

"I was a jealous fool," he began. "You deserve so much more in a man than what I have to offer. I'm ashamed for doubting you and I apologize for treating you badly. I love you. I know you can't forgive me, but I had to let you know how I feel. I've been a jackass, but I had never encountered someone like you before. You are honest and loyal, but I was always thinking you would see how flawed I am and realize being with me was a mistake. So I brushed you off before I could let you hurt me. But I hurt us in the process."

Viv had never heard Jamal speak with so much emotion and depth before. She knew he had a sensitive side, but hadn't realized how deeply he must have been hurt in the past. She had always wondered why when they were getting closer, Jamal would draw back and retreat into his shell.

Vivian Looked deeply into Jamal's eyes and said, "I am not your past. I realize now that you have trust issues, and I'm sorry for that. But you need to see me, really see me for the person I am, the woman who has been in your corner, your biggest cheerleader. And what you do have to offer me is what I have always wanted…your love. I'm not going to sit here and pretend everything is okay with us because you opened up to me, or that we will never have a disagreement. Loving someone should not be hard, but it sometimes is. I know that it is not always 50/50. It was Marvin Gaye who said it's sometimes a 70/30 love."

"Baby," Jamal replied, "I believe we have something strong enough to build a future on if you can believe in me again. I should never have doubted you. You are a good woman. Can you take this fool back?"

With that said the two embraced. Viv could feel the tension draining from Jamal. He raised her chin and planted a soft kiss on her lips that deepened from a hunger and longing they both felt. "Baby steps," Viv murmured as they broke apart. "Anything you say," was Jamal's husky reply as thy sat comfortably together.

"Let me cook dinner for you tomorrow, Viv. I do have some culinary skills to show off. Can you come over at 7? We do need to spend more time together."

"Alright," Viv replied. "Do you need me to bring anything? A bottle of wine?"

"No, just bring your sweet self."

"Okay, but I've got to help Angel now so we can wrap up for the evening."

With their relationship on the upswing now, Jamal appeared as if a boulder had dropped from his shoulders. Vivian knew there was much work ahead for the two of them, but she felt that she and Jamal had what it took to form a loving, fulfilling relationship and become a power couple to reckon with. Tomorrow night Viv would bring up couples counseling and hope that he would see that as a favorable step for their relationship. Viv wanted marriage in the future that would last. She was sure that with emotional intervention they could achieve all they could ever aspire to.

Across town Paul and Monique finally put closure on a few issues. He had been having a hard time trying to wrap his head around the fact that he had a 9-year-old son with Monique. She had not told him of the baby she was expecting while he was rehabbing from his injuries connected with Angelique's kidnapping. They had broken up during that time and after recuperating and hearing no word on Angel, Paul returned to school, a semester late. Monique's family moved from their hometown when her father received a job promotion before the baby was born. Monique had her child, returned to school and severed all ties with Paul. There was no way he would ever have found out about his child if he had not run into her by chance downtown. The child at her side bore a strong resemblance to Paul when he was that age.

Paul's suspicions were confirmed later when Monique agreed to meet him for coffee at a small café near his law office. He was visibly upset at having the knowledge of his son, Jon, kept from him for so long, but he managed to control his anger. To her credit, Monique was remorseful. She had not kept Jon a secret out of revenge.

"I thought I was doing the right thing after we broke up. You said you were in love with someone else, and I didn't want you to return to me out of obligation."

"I understand how you must have felt, but didn't you think I should have at least been told about him? I deserved that much. I've missed so many years!"

"I'm truly sorry. I wasn't trying to hurt you. At first I was confused and hurt. My parents said I should tell you, but I just couldn't at the time. And as time passed it got harder and harder. And I thought by now you would have married and had a family of your own. Please forgive me."

With those sincere words of apology from Monique some of the sting was gone for Paul. But he still had many questions, including why she had not told him of Jon's existence sometime after running into each other at the black-tie affair. Their meeting had been purely by chance as Monique had accompanied another guest that evening. Paul reminded himself too that he had gone as Angel's escort and that was neither the time nor place for such a personal conversation. But what had Monique told Jon about his father? He definitely wanted a role in his son's life. It was not in Paul's nature to turn his back on a child of his, no matter the circumstance.

It was only in the past year that Monique had moved to the area for work. She had no idea that Paul lived anywhere near the metropolitan Washington, DC area. Fate seemed to have played a cruel trick on her. But it was time she faced the ghosts of her past. In truth, Paul had been her first love since they were children in kindergarten. There are no guarantees in life, however. She and Paul had never talked about marriage, but they had been a couple for so long that it was assumed by both families that they would marry after undergraduate school. Monique didn't want Paul to stay with her because of a child and grow to resent her. She knew he would postpone finishing school and maybe never make it to law school, as was his plan.

"I told Jon that his father lived far away. I never said anything bad about you."

"I appreciate that, but I would like to get to know him, be a part of his life from here on. This hasn't been fair to Jon or me."

"You're right, but give me some time to let me tell him about you first. Then you can come by and meet him."

"I want to do more than meet him. I want to build a relationship with him as his father regardless of who is in your life now. Did you even list me as his father on his birth certificate?"

"Yes, I did. But I didn't think our paths would ever cross again. Neither of us lived in this town."

"I see you thought of everything, except fate or chance. Let's not let this become ugly. I don't mean you any ill will. We were friends and more for far too long."

"I know, and you're right. We owe it to Jon to keep things amicable. I'll call you after I've told him who you are."

~

Max's stay in Tahiti proved very informative. He learned that the vintage bracelet left behind when Angel was kidnapped came from Jamari Dupre's collection, none other than Angel's father. This piece of evidence had not been revealed to the public, but Max's resource not only knew about the bracelet, but also what was inscribed on the underside of the bracelet, *My First Love*. This was especially telling as it was inscribed in the Berber language, a Tamazight dialect. This is why a forensics analyst was needed. However, the bracelet disappeared from holding before it could be translated. Max knew Jamari had ties to the Berber people through his ancestry. This accounted for the exotic appearance of Angel. If he could only put the pieces together!

But why would Jamari kidnap his own daughter and have her subjected to such awful circumstances, and for so long, Max mused. There had to be something he was missing in this intricate web that was developing. From everything he had learned about Angel's ordeal, she hadn't been mistreated. Quite the opposite after her initial capture. But getting much information from her had been almost impossible. She never revealed anything about her captors, claiming she couldn't remember after being given a clean bill of health from the hospital.

Once reunited with Michelle, Angel just wanted to put the nightmare behind her. Her wounds were not physical, but psychological trauma is a different story entirely. No one wanted to push Angel too hard. Healing was what she needed most. After all, she had missed most of her senior year of high school. But with private tutoring, Angel made up for the time lost, and managed to graduate with honors the following school year. But the bubbly, confident young woman was long gone. Angel returned withdrawn, and it had taken years of therapy for her to become the mature, strong, and resilient woman she was today.

Max was more determined than ever now to connect the dots… Raphael Medici, Jamari Dupre, Paul Monroe, Michelle Dupre and possibly Jack Montenero…What was he missing? A late-night call once Max returned from Tahiti held all the missing pieces to the puzzle. Now he knew the truth. But could he, should he reveal this information to Angel now that she had found peace in her life? Would it have any bearing on the life she had made for herself? He could and would definitely reveal Paul's innocent involvement. But how could he reveal that and withhold the rest? Max was in a quandary!

~

It was now time to step back from the Vivian / Jamal saga that Angel had been drawn into. True, she had a minor role in getting the two back into the same orbit, but now that they were communicating, she would be hands off. Besides, Angel had her own issues with the publishing company, the attentions of Edward Morgan and her unresolved feelings and concerns centered on Paul Monroe. If she was completely honest with herself, Angel did care for Edward, but she was not in love with him.

Although Edward would be a great catch as he was kind, loving and would be an excellent provider, he did not elicit the same reaction in Angel that Paul did. Sparks did not ignite for Angel in Edward's company as they did when she was around Paul. Angel was mature enough to know you can't base a relationship purely on attraction, though. But there it was. Her heart would flip-flop in Paul's presence, and in close contact she couldn't think straight.

It was 10:30 on a sunny Saturday morning, the weekend following the celebrated fund raiser and fashion show, when Angel opened her front door to allow Paul entry. He had called earlier in the week asking to speak with her privately on a serious matter, and the heaviness in his voice alarmed yet intrigued her at the same time. The hoped-for joy in his voice, present during the first time he presented himself on her doorstop, was missing this time. His eyes held a trace of something she couldn't quite discern. Wariness? Sadness? Angel had been ready to say no to his request, but thought better of it. It was time to hopefully uncover the truth about the mysterious Monique and Paul's sudden appearance at the ski chalet where they first met.

"Let's sit on my deck out back," Angel said. "The weather is perfect today." Soft instrumental music was piped throughout the house and could be softly heard on the deck through discretely placed speakers.

"I can offer you cranberry orange muffins, a sweet strawberry Moscato wine or iced tea if you prefer," murmured Angel.

"Thanks, a muffin and wine would be great," Paul replied.

Angel's preparations would give him a moment to collect himself as he sat on a cushioned deck chair patterned in a riot of orange colored blossoms. A large overhead umbrella provided the perfect shield from the intense rays of the sun. Paul took in the bubbling brook that coursed through the back of the property and the small garden of summer flowers. The scent of wild honeysuckle and flowering blooms, caught on the wind, intoxicated Paul's senses.

He understood why Angel chose this spot to talk. He could envision her out here writing the stories and articles that had made her famous. This location lent an air of tranquility to an otherwise nervous situation for Paul. He wrestled with telling Angel of his child, Jon, fearing this information and the timeline might cause her to further mistrust him. Paul had come this far, though. There was no turning back if he ever hoped to rekindle Angel's trust and affection for him.

~

As Angelique submitted to the ministrations of the masseuse at her local spa Angel thought to herself, "Can I really believe the tale Paul told me this morning?" She now knew who the beautiful Monique Dubois was, and was rightfully shocked to learn of Paul's son. He had seemed sincere and Angel realized that to learn of something so life changing could be devasting, even if it was a good thing. The news saddened Angel for another reason, though. It opened up the ache for her daughter, Kimmie, who would be a few years younger than Jon if she had lived. Could she believe that Paul was really going to tell her of his girlfriend at another college and his need to break up with this young woman that fateful day when she was abducted? It was plausible, if memory served her correctly.

Angle's last moments and conversation with Paul so many years ago stuck in her memory and had plagued her for years. The last thing she remembered was Paul saying he was sorry, then darkness came from her abductors who chloroformed her. No, she could believe the part about Monique and the child, but Angel was conflicted over Paul's story. Had he deliberately lured her to the woods that early morning ten years ago? Was he saying sorry for what was about to happen to her? Or sorry for not revealing he had a love interest?

"I'll wait to hear from Max when he returns from his long overdue vacation," reasoned Angel aloud as she dressed to leave the spa. With a free afternoon Angel decided to just take a long drive in the warm sunshine and enjoy the beautiful weather. Often these drives lent inspiration to articles and stories that Angel would develop. As she drove around a winding bend in the road, oddly deserted at this hour, Angel's cell phone chimed. She quickly tapped her console to answer the call coming in from her dear friend, Captain Maxwell Franklin.

"This is a pleasant surprise," quipped Angel. "But aren't you supposed to be on vacation?

"I am," replied Max, but I flew back home a few days early. Will you have time to meet me day after tomorrow? I have some news for you."

"Absolutely," replied Angel. "Just name the place and time."

"Will 11:30 work for you? We can meet at Panera Bread and have a bite to eat. I don't mind mixing business with pleasure. And Angel, breathe."

Angel could hear the smile in Max's voice and readily agreed with a chuckle. His was the call she had been hoping for, but had no idea it would come so soon. Angel so wanted to believe Paul and to believe in him. There was no question that she would be accepting of his son. But would Monique be agreeable to the inevitable relationship Angel would have with Jon if Paul came back into her life? Was a relationship with Paul even possible after the years apart? The meeting with Max would take place in two days. Finally she would get the answers she so desperately needed, and could now compare Paul's account to what Max uncovered. Turning her car around at the next turn-about Angel headed for home.

Two days had passed and now Angel sat directly across from Maxwell Franklin nursing a hot cup of mint tea while nibbling at a turkey sandwich and air fried chips. This man held the answers to so many questions Angel had had for so long. A knot was forming in her stomach as Max sat attempting banter. Any other time Angel would have enjoyed sparring with Max, but now she dreaded, yet anxiously anticipated, the report awaiting her. But Max insisted on them enjoying their meals first before divulging anything having to do with business. And as Max had refused any payment for his services and information, Angel was determined to be patient. Max insisted he had been due a long overdue and much needed vacation. It had been no trouble for him to combine uncovering the facts Angel desired while enjoying his time in Tahiti.

Now that the meeting had concluded and Angel was safely secluded in her cozy den, she had time to reflect on the intoxicating developments Max had disclosed at their brunch. She had not been aware of Her mother's, Michelle's, first love, her dad's brother. Nor did she know about any of the business dealings of her father, Jamari, or Jack Montenero, who became her stepdad after her kidnapping. To further complicate the picture was Raphael Medici and his connection to Paul as his godfather. Max had laid out a diabolical yet intriguing plan of events that revolved around desire, deception and revenge.

Since Angel's mother and Jack had passed away she could not verify any of Max's conclusions on that front. And Paul would not have any knowledge of Raphael's malicious intent over the loss of his love, Serita, Paul's mother. What was even more confounding was Raphael Medici blaming Jack for Paul meeting Serita, his former business partner. This was a case of mislaid blame that had festered until it boiled over into a diabolical plan that backfired when Angel had been mistakenly snatched instead of her mother. She was sure Raphael intended to inflict pain on Jack Montenero by snatching Michelle during their skiing vacation.

This monster made sure Paul was working at the ski lodge so he could inconspicuously gather intel on Jack and Michelle. Worse was the fact that her uncle, Damien, who never knew of Angel's existence, had been forced to get involved with Raphael's scheme. Damien owed a large debt to Raphael who took Damien's very expensive antique silver bracelet as collateral. It was no mistake that the bracelet had been left behind to implicate Damien and Jamari. Damien was told only that he would be guarding *cargo* on the partially deserted island. That *cargo* turned out to be the niece he had never met!

Angel had been pouring over the dossier for hours when she finally made the connection between Damien and Jamari, her father. The puzzle pieces began to fit. Jamari is the younger brother of Damien who never returned home. Damien and Michelle had been engaged. Damien discovered from friends that his brother, Jamari, has married Michelle, Damien's fiancé. Damien is then so devastated from the news that he never returned home. The truth: Angel's father,

Jamari, had convinced Michelle that Damien was dead. Jamari had lied, saying his brother had been killed while fighting as a mercenary in a coup in Turkey.

Angel now realized why this silent, brooding man had been convinced she was lying about her identity the first time Damien saw her. Losing Michelle to Jamari through a lie had been an unbearable betrayal. Damien didn't know Angel existed. She resembled her mother and could have been her mother's double. But Angel couldn't dwell on that fact. She now realized that even though Damien had been forced to *guard cargo*, he hadn't participated in her abduction. He never had any ill intent for her mother, and by association, her. Angel now understood that Damien had protected her as he would have Michelle because she was his niece and the child he had hoped to have with Michelle. Now she understood Damien's initial frustration. He had only acted with kindness towards her on the island. She now wondered if he had had a part in her rescue.

The shrill ring of the cell phone interrupted Angel's thoughts. "Well, I need a little diversion," she said to no one. It was Edward. She had been avoiding him, and feigned a busy work schedule to put him off a few days ago. In truth, Angle wanted time to review the papers in the dossier Max had left with her with no interruptions. It seemed that would be impossible. Her friendships were important to her. Angel wanted to be there for them as they were always there for her.

"How are you my darlin'?" Edward crooned. "Do you think you can squeeze in a little time for me today?"

"Of course," replied Michelle, even though her mind was elsewhere. "What did you have in mind?"

"How about I fix us dinner at my place around 6:00 and then we take in a movie at the Arundel Mills Cinemark? There are a couple of good movies playing," Edward replied.

"That does sound nice," Angel replied. "I could use a break and I can't think of anyone else I'd rather have fun with right now."

This was true. The jury was still out on Paul. Angel would need to pour over the documents pertaining to Paul and the other people Max had privately and secretly investigated. She wanted to act solely on information, not emotion this time around where Paul was concerned. A night out would do Angel good. She figured this would allow her to clear her mind and refocus on her task at hand with a clear head. Angel began to rummage through her closet for something to wear, but before she could decide on an outfit her phone rang again.

"I have wonderful news," gushed Viv. "You know that Jamal and I are in a really good place now. Well, he took me to diner last night and he popped the question. He asked me to marry him, and I said yes!"

"Wow!," exclaimed Angel. "This seems sudden, but I'm happy for you."

"Thanks girl!" and then Viv whispered, "I owe it all to you and the fund-raising event. Jamal isn't really the jealous type. But he was insecure and holding onto baggage from a past relationship that had gone sour. Therapy has helped us both tremendously."

"I'm glad it worked out for you both," said Angel.

"Thanks," said Viv, "but the other reason I'm calling is to ask you to be my Maid of Honor at my wedding. Will you?"

"Yes, of course. If you asked someone else I'd be upset," quipped Angel. "I know you haven't decided on a date yet, but let me know when."

"Actually, we have," said Vivian. "We want a small wedding, just our close friends in attendance for the ceremony. My father is securing the Country Club for the third Saturday next month."

"What! So soon? How did you manage that?" asked Angel.

"Jamal had already spoken to my father, the little sneak, and dad had made some calls in case I said yes. Jamal always knew I never wanted a large wedding. But get prepared for the reception. That's going to be a blow out!"

"So. I'm losing my partner in crime in a month! Well, I'm happy for you and willing to help if you need anything," replied Angel.

"As a matter of fact, I do. You can help me pick out a wedding dress. My mom and dad are handling everything else, thank goodness. Even though the wedding will be small, I want to dazzle Jamal and everybody else when I make my entrance at the reception."

After a bit more chit chat the call concluded. Vivian had to line up bridal boutiques and appointments for the two of them to visit in search of a spectacular gown. Booking appointments would be no problem for the well-connected Vivian Summervale, soon to be Mrs. Jamal Leonard. No, the appointments would be no problem. But Angel knew picking out a gown would be a monumental task. Even though Viv had model proportions and could look good in a rag, she was meticulous to a point. But that's why the two were such good friends. Angel had a level head and would steer Vivian to make a great choice in gowns as money was no object for the Summervales.

Vivian's life seemed to be on the course she set out for herself. Marriage to Jamal would be like putting the cherry on the top of a cake. The two really were made for each other, complemented each other, and in Angel's opinion, would make a great power couple with the strengths they both brought to the table. Now Angel just had to sort out her own life. Yes, she was successful in her career pursuit, but she was still missing her *other half*, someone she loved and who loved her in return, someone whom she could completely trust with her heart this time. Someone who wanted her for herself alone. With those thoughts running through her head, Angel smiled and stepped into her walk-in closet to adorn herself for the casual evening ahead with Edward Morgan.

Edward had chef qualities when it came to the kitchen. This was something Angel had become quite fond of in him. He could whip up a delicacy from practically nothing. And Angel was the recipient of many of his taste test delights. But Edward wanted more than friendship and although Angel really cared for Edward, loved him actually, she wasn't in love with him. Would caring be enough or would she be short-changing both of them?

"I really enjoyed myself this evening Eddy," Angel affectionately stated as she and Edward exited the theater.

"I did too, but I always enjoy myself when I'm around you," Edward replied. "The night is still young. Would you like to come back to my place for a brandy?"

Angel could see the desire in Edward's eyes but she had to be true to herself and decline. "I wish I could, but I have a few articles to proof before sending them to my publisher. Raincheck?"

"Always," replied Edward, but Angel could detect hurt in his voice and saw less sparkle in his eyes. Angel remained upbeat on the ride to her place, but Eddy was quieter than usual. As they pulled up to her house Ed turned to Angel and took one of her hands in his.

"You know I really care for you Angel. I was hoping you felt the same for me."

"I do care for you Eddy, but I'm wrestling with a few things right now. I'm trying to be fair to both of us. Please be patient with me a little longer."

"I'm trying," Eddy said, "but you must know how much you mean to me."

It was time for more truth, so Angel plunged in.

"I'm conflicted, in truth. Someone from my past has shown up and we never had closure. I need to work through this. I don't believe in playing games. That's why I'm telling you this."

This was hard for Eddy to hear but he respected hearing the truth from Angel. He planted a kiss on the inside of her palm after walking her to her door and said goodnight. In retrospect, Angel mused, the night could have gone badly after her revelation. But Eddy was a true gentleman and friend. But she knew Edward didn't want to be in the friend zone. Angel needed to decide if she wanted to see if there was any hope for her and Paul, whom she knew was more than willing. Paul had made that clear on his last visit.

"Ugh! It's raining men," Angel said aloud as she closed the door and leaned her back against it. Edward. Maxwell. Paul. "It's always either a wasteland or a floodgate of men!" Angel also secretly knew Max was crushing on her but she never let on that she knew. Where is true love?

The next few weeks were uneventful. Angel threw herself into deciphering and following the leads the information Max's scrutiny pointed to. Angel even reached out to her father, Jamari. This was difficult as the two hadn't talked in years. Theirs's had been a strained relationship for quite some time after her abduction and her mother's passing. It was clear Jamari had been flooded with grief on hearing Angel was missing, although he had never been overly affectionate with her as a child. But Angel was no longer a child or young adult. She needed answers without prying too deeply into her parents' personal lives. To get the answers she required Angel knew she would have to have a face-to-face with her dad. This way she could look him in his eyes to determine if he was telling the truth or not. A phone call could only do so much.

"I'll have some free time soon, Dad," she said softly into the phone. I'd like to fly out to see you. It's been a long time since we've seen each other, and I am your only child."

Jamari hesitated but the guilt-trip worked. "Are you certain you can get away? I know how busy you can be."

It sounded like her dad was trying to avoid a confrontation which would definitely happen if he remained cagey. Instead she kept a level head.

"No Dad, I can always make time for you."

Angel was sure this shocked Jamari, but no way could he now refuse to meet with her. They talked a few minutes more and Angel got Jamari to commit to meeting with her at his Miami location in two weeks. Miami was the perfect urban city for Jamari's thriving import export business, as this was an exceptionally diverse city. Miami was home to a vibrant art scene, with several art shows, galleries and museums throughout the city. Angel also knew the stunning beaches, outstanding restaurants and exciting social scene was what drew Jamari to Miami more than the other cities he had businesses in.

Her Dad was by nature reserved. He had never been one to call attention to himself, but he enjoyed being where the action was. And Jamari also loved being in the company of beautiful women. This was not a hard feat for him. Jamari was quite a handsome man possessing a full head of luxurious chestnut brown hair with natural auburn highlights. He was also athletically toned and looked years younger than his actual 51 years. In truth, Angel could only speculate that she was his only child, or at least the only one he outwardly recognized. She kept this thought to herself as she rang off with, *Bye Daddy*, words not spoken in years.

Angel knew her *missing dad syndrome* played heavily into the type of men she was drawn to. They were usually very confident but somehow just out of reach emotionally. Angel chalked this deficit in them up to their childhoods and she had had enough of damaged or callous men for a lifetime. Now there were two confirmed good guys: Edward and Max, with Paul as a possible third. The doorbell rang. The face on the other side of the doorway was obliterated by the sumptuous array of red roses held out to her. And there was Paul smiling shyly down on her. He was gorgeous with his sun-kissed, tanned face behind sunglasses that couldn't hide the mirth in his eyes.

"Am I too early?" Paul asked spying Angel in her lounging pjs.

"Oh my gosh!" Angel exclaimed, taking the flowers he held out. "These are beautiful." She had completely forgotten she had agreed to Paul's invitation to a concert in the park.

"Come in. I won't be but a few minutes. I'll just put these beauties in water. I'm so sorry! I completely forgot you were coming over. I'll be ready in a sec," she said as she dashed into her kitchen for a vase and then up her stairs to quickly change.

Angel had showered earlier so she just needed to freshen up and change into her favorite pair of white jeans, a frilly fuchsia print blouse and wedge heel sandals. Angel planned to relax and see where things would go. Now that Paul was here she decided to discreetly question him on the drive to the concert. There were a few things she had uncovered in Max's report that puzzled her. Today was as good a day as any to move forward in getting to the truth of the events that lead to her abduction.

More questions about Monique and Jon, Paul's son, came to the forefront, but Angel knew she had to tread lightly in that department. For some time now Angel had the uneasy feeling that someone was watching her whenever she was in a crowded situation. She desperately wanted to be able to finally put her harrowing ordeal behind her in order to be free to live her life without constantly looking over her shoulder. To do this she needed not only Paul's truth about himself and Raphael Medici, but also Jamari's part, if any, in what happened to her that horrific Spring ten years ago and her rescue. The last nugget that would tie everything up neatly was Damien, her long-lost uncle. She was positive Jamari didn't know she knew about him. That would soon change.

Even though Paul and Angel hadn't spent any substantial time together in ten years, save the limited time he eventually helped her with legal matters, Angel found herself surprisingly comfortable in his company. Much had happened in both their lives over the intervening years, but basically Paul seemed to be the same person she had met years ago. She had been drawn to him as a teen, and those same feelings kept bubbling to the surface. Angel shifted in her seat as they drove to the park grounds, physically pushing these thoughts and feelings aside, and began to enjoy herself.

The weather was perfect, not humid but warm with a slight breeze rustling through the surrounding trees. Paul had come prepared with two camp chairs and a small cooler with ice cold beverages and chips. There was electricity in the air in anticipation for the music to begin. The Earth, Wind and Fire Tribute Band was on the venue along with several other great acts, free for all attendees. The final artist to perform was Ledisi, and by then the crowd was standing and fiercely clapping to encourage her to the stage.

At the end of the night Angel and Paul found themselves hoarse from singing along with all the acts, but it was a sweet culmination to the evening under the stars. After relaxing and becoming one with nature and music Angel determined this was the perfect time to subtly inquire about Monique and Jon.

"I know I have no right to ask, but are you still involved with Monique?" Angel asked. This seemed a safe segue leading to other more complicated questions.

"No, I hadn't seen her since college. But now that Jon is in the picture I plan to be active in his life," Paul responded. "If you think this will change how I feel about you, you have nothing to worry about."

"I'm actually glad to hear you want to be a part of his life; I admire you for stepping up," Angel replied.

"I only wish I had found out sooner," Paul said somberly. "I can't make up for time that has passed, but Jon is still young enough for us to bond; he deserves a father."

Angel was bursting with pride at these words and hesitated only momentarily before delving into the events of their last day in the snow-filled woods. "Paul, how did you happen to be working at the ski chalet where we met? Jack was a stickler for privacy, and you weren't on the list of employees presented to him," Angel huskily murmured.

Paul looked up sharply at Angel then down at the steering wheel where he sat before answering. Paul had pulled over, stopping in a clearing where the stars twinkled brightly in the heavens. Three heartbeats turned to five before he responded. "Angel, I'm not sure where this is coming from, but let me assure you, I had no involvement in the events of that day." Taking a breath, he began to relay to Angel the why and how he happened to be working at the ski chalet.

As he recalled the events surrounding his impromptu hiring, first being told no, then yes at the mention of his godfather, Raphael Medici, Angel settled in to absorb it all. At the end of his account Angel seemed satisfied with his retelling of the events, but she could not shake the feeling that some part had been left out. She was not to find out this night, but secrets kept hidden eventually do come to light.

As Paul walked Angel to her door she let her hand linger in his. He took this as a sign that she was steadily warming up to him. Before she could put her key in the lock he tipped up her face with his index finger, staring adoringly into her eyes. He could feel the heat of desire radiating from her, but decided to not come on too strong. Baby steps. He brushed the hair from her face and cradled her head, planting the softest kiss on her lips. The kiss deepened with them both losing track of all time and space. Angel moved into Paul's embrace and for just a moment they were both transported back in time to a sweeter period. For Angel it was a time of longing and awakening, for Paul it was recognition of deep feelings for Angel. Feelings that he had never felt for Monique. It soared above lust, though that was definitely mingled into the mix for them both.

Shakily Angel withdrew from Paul with swollen lips from the pleasurable sensations of the kiss. Catching her breath Angel demurely spoke into Paul's chest.

"Duty calls," she cried. "I have a heavy workload this week with much to finish before I go out of town for a few days."

Taking the hint, Paul took a step back, retrieved Angel's keys from her and deftly opened her door for her.

"Alright," he replied. "Don't burn the candle at both ends. I need you to save some time for me."

At that, Angel smiled, gave Paul a hug and quickly entered her condo. She said goodnight and shut the door before she could change her mind. As tempting as it was to be in Paul's arms, Angel felt deep in her core there was a missing piece to Paul's story. "Patience," she uttered with her back to the door, "and resolve." Miami and Jamari were just a few days away. More doors to open in the mystery.

Jamari

It had been quite a few years since Angel had stood face to face with Jamari, the man who she share half of her DNA with. Her father. She had only seen him two or three times since her parents divorced when she was around five or six. He was basically a stranger, yet held blood ties to her forever. This bond is what Angelique relied on when she uttered the words, *Daddy*, on her phone call to him. It had the desired effect. Jamari agreed to meet with her and now Angel stood in the terminal of the Fort Lauderdale-Hollywood International Airport, having just made her way through security. This was the closest airport to Miami. Angel stepped into the heat of the Florida air and scanned the drivers holding placards. As if on cue one of the drivers stepped forward and addressed her.

"Ms. Dupre, may I take your bags?"

"How did you know I'm Ms. Dupre," Angel uttered, wide eyed in disbelief." Officially her last name was still Sterling for publication recognition.

"Madam, your picture graces your father's walls. I am Alvaro. I am to take you to the Aventura Ranch on Highland Lakes Boulevard, at your father's instructions. It's just ten miles away."

Angel knew this was not too far from the Adrienne Arsht Center for the Performing Arts. From her research of the area Angel discovered it was formerly known as the Carnival Center, but was renamed for the philanthropist who donated $30 million to the facility to make it financially stable. She hoped to take in a performance before she returned home. However, she had half expected to stay at her father's home. Alvaro must have picked up on Angel's shifting mood and the slight frown on her face. He quickly responded.

"Mr. Dupre felt you would be more comfortable there as he has given his staff vacation leave at this time. If you will allow me."

Alvaro was standing with the proffered door open to the Lincoln Continental. With one last glance around Angel stepped into the backseat of the luxury car and leaned back, settling in for what she hoped would be a short ride. Seemingly just moments later, Angel found herself heavy lidded and drowsing on the backseat. It took a few moments for her to realize the car had stopped. Alvaro already had her luggage on the curb and was holding his hand to help her from the vehicle.

"Mr. Dupre asked me to tell you that he will be tied up with some business affairs until 6:00, but if you are able he would like you to join him for dinner at 7:00. A car will be sent for you."

"That will be fine," Angel responded, welcoming a few hours to get settled and rest before the evening. Being cooped up on a flight even for just a few hours, always took a toll on Angel.

"Alvaro is rather an exotic name isn't it?" queried Angel as she stepped from the car. "What does it mean?"

The stocky driver smiled and slightly dipped his head before answering. "It means cautious, senora," Alvaro replied. Angel would be wise to remember this. Usually names and their meanings imprint on the owner.

"I'll bring your bags to your room, Ms. Dupre," Alvaro said, as he handed her the keys to the villa. "I procured your keys for you as Mr. Dupre instructed. Please enjoy your stay here in Miami." With that said Alvaro grabbed the suitcase handles as Angel took the short walk to her bedroom suite, one of five, on the ground floor. There was a casino on site, but Angel had no interest in gambling, even for fun.

What she relished right now was a warm shower to wash away the travel and a quick nap. The same temperature here in Florida felt so much hotter and draining than at home. Hopefully after this night she could convince her father to let her share his domicile for her brief stay in Miami.

Jamari's car arrived precisely at 6:30 that evening. Angelique had donned a backless white pantsuit with a plunging yet not too revealing neckline and carried a peach colored shawl. She was prepared to ward off the chill inside the restaurant. Angel decided to wear low heel shoes in case the opportunity for a stroll should present itself. As if on cue, Jamari emerged from the car just as Angel exited the villa. His head came up as Angel walked toward him with an expression she couldn't fathom. He reached for Angel's hand and enfolded her in a fatherly hug. Tears sprang to the corner of his eyes and he quickly brushed them away.

"It's been too long, my Angel," Jamari said with a husky voice. Angel hugged her father back, but wasn't prepared for the emotions that surfaced between the two of them. "I'm glad to see you, Dad," Angel softly intoned. Jamari was deeply moved at the sight of his 'little girl' whom he had not seen in years.

"You've got me here for two weeks, Dad. But right now I'm famished," Angel said with a smile. The mood needed to lighten up and with that said Jamari held the car door for his daughter.

"I'll let you choose tonight. Do you have a preference? I can recommend places that serve excellent Cuban, Greek, or American fare.

"I haven't had really good Greek food in a long while. Can we do that?" Angel asked.

"Of course," said Jamari. "Alvaro, it's going to be Santorini tonight."

"Yes sir," said Alvaro. We should be there in twenty minutes."

With that said the two rode in comfortable silence to the restaurant, with Jamari holding one of Angel's hands in his hands the entire time. Angel and Jamari were seated right away at a cozy spot outside to enjoy the breezes. Their meals, a fusion of Mediterranean and Greek flavors, arrived promptly and were delicious. Jamari seemed to be so happy each time Angel referred to him as *Dad*. It was obvious he was proud of his daughter, but perhaps he was buoyed with the endearment because he had kept his distance from her and had not regularly communicated with her. To her credit, Angel was sincere in her feelings toward her dad. A part of her still looked for his approval even if she didn't fully trust her feelings with him.

As dinner ended Jamari suggested they walk along the beach since it was a beautiful evening and not yet late. Angel agreed. She wanted to begin to establish a father / daughter relationship not just to get truthful answers about her kidnapping, but because this was her dad, the only parent she had. After walking a short distance they found a nearby bench. Jamari began to mend the breach that existed.

"I have not been there for you when you needed me most and I'm sorry. You have been through so much in such a short period of time and I retreated," Jamari stated. "I can do better, and I want to."

"I appreciate your honesty, Dad; that means more than you can imagine," replied Angel. "I want us to become closer."

"Me too," replied Jamari. "Are you comfortable at Aventura Ranch?"

"It's very nice, but I'd rather stay with you, help or no help," Angel replied. "I'm not picky. Can you make that happen, Daddy?

This request tore at Jamari's heartstrings, especially when she said *Daddy*.

"Give me a day to take care of a few things and I'll make it happen. I want you to be happy," Jamari said giving her shoulder a hug. "I've been away; I just came back in town today and need to get my place tip top and fill my refrigerator."

"Okay," said Angel, "I can live with that, Daddy."

They chatted a while longer, getting Jamari up to speed on her career and her newest novel that she and her agent were promoting. In turn, Jamari told Angel a bit about his import-export business and the direction he saw it going. He even hinted that maybe one day if she wanted to, she might work with him. After a series of poorly muffled yawns from Angel, Jamari suggested he call Alvaro to take Angel back to the villa to get a good night sleep. There would be more times to get together during the next two weeks.

True to his word, Jamari managed to ready his home for Angelique to join him and stocked up on delicacies she may want to nibble on. He was adept in the kitchen, so on her first night with him he prepared a sumptuous Italian feast beginning with ossobuco and a side of risotto that would rival that of the best chef. In truth, Jamari had studied cuisine and had once worked as a chef for a very prestigious establishment. This was how he raised money to start his own import-export business. Now he would use his culinary skills to delight his daughter. Or so he hoped.

He would start to soften her toward him through her stomach. Jamari was not naïve to think Angel held no anger against him for practically abandoning her as a child. It was true she and her mother moved thousands of miles away, but he didn't give Michelle any reason to stay in a dead marriage. He could and should have given more thought to Angel, especially in her formative years. Jamari couldn't turn the clock back, but he was determined to change their relationship for the better going forward.

Miami was a beautiful and exciting city allowing Angel to forget some of the worries in her life. Jamari enlightened her on the various aspects of the city, reminding her that Miami was the third richest city in the U.S. from a 2018 study of 77 world cities by the UBS, a Swiss multinational investment bank. This fact was vital for the success of Jamari's business. Where there was wealth there was opportunity to grow his business. Plus, Miami had one of the busiest ports for passenger traffic and cruise lines. All this meant potential customers and clients for his ever-thriving business which he had successfully expanded exponentially.

After several days of relaxing on the beach, soaking up the sun and enjoying some of the night life with her father, Angel had a heart to heart with Jamari concerning her kidnappers and the players in that horrific scenario. She recounted to her father what she remembered of her ordeal and was rewarded with additional details Jamari had uncovered. Angel already knew from Max of the ruthless and ridiculous vendetta Raphael Medici held for Jack Montenero and why. From Jamari she learned that Raphael had his tentacles into her father's business as a silent and unknown investor. Because of a dispute, Raphael was determined to exact revenge on Jamari by implicating him and his brother. Only Raphael's plan backfired when the wrong person, Angelique, was captured.

~

Now that Angel had returned home she needed time to decompress and sort things out. There was much on Angel's mind from all she learned and experienced during her time in Miami with Jamari, her father. The trip to see him had been cathartic for Angel. She was able to excise some of the demons she had concerning her dad being *missing in action* when she was young. Although Angel asked some very explicit questions concerning Jamari's life with her mother, Michelle, she didn't bother asking Jamari about Damien, her uncle, as Max had given her the highlights on Damien and Jamari's relationship. She did find out though that through a message Damien managed to send to Jamari he was able to put things in motion for Angel's rescue.

Raphael had been expert at covering his tracks, so there was no actual physical evidence linking him to the kidnapping. However, Maxwell's investigation, though off the books, had uncovered an unlawful operation leaving a trail of money laundering. With this information now in the hands of law enforcement it was only a matter of time before Raphael would be behind bars, serving a lengthy sentence. He had already been arrested and was awaiting trial. Angel was delighted that this vengeful man was about to lose his freedom, but she still had lingering suspicions about Paul and his involvement with Raphael.

For the time being Angel would have to step out of the role of amateur detective and into the role of Maid of Honor for Vivian. The appointments for bridal gowns had been made at several locations, with the next one in a couple of days. During this down time Angel had time to mull over some holes in her abduction tale. She still suspected Paul had withheld something of his role from her during their last encounter. What, if any information, had Paul given to Raphael or his goons? Jack had excellent security, but Angel had to admit she and Paul had eluded them most of the vacation. Something was amiss. Angel's room had been tossed so whoever the culprit, it was intentional. And meant for her. A quick phone call to Jamari was in order to confirm her suspicions.

Viv and Jamal's intimate wedding went off without a hitch. Just a select number of family and friends were in attendance at the Summervale home for the nuptials. True to form, the reception at the country club was exquisite. Unsure of Paul and his motivations, coupled with her suspicions, Angel invited Edward as her plus one. She had to risk the implications of inviting Eddy to the wedding. Those on the outside would look on Eddy as Angel's significant other from the way he looked at her whenever she came near him. With her uncertainty of Paul, Angel was leaning more and more toward Edward. He sincerely cared for her, was stable and dependable, and always had her best interests at heart. Angel's plans for herself included a husband and eventually a family. She already had a thriving career. Plus, Eddy's mom was from Morocco so they had cultural heritage in common.

Pulling herself out of her reverie, Angel smiled and posed as the photographer took pictures of the wedding party. This happy event took Angel back to happier times. She missed being a mother. This is part of what motivated her to find real true love this time. She saw a great example in her mother, Michelle and Jack, her stepfather. Theirs was a friendship, a partnership and a love relationship that ended only due to a tragic accident. Her daughter, Kimmie, was the light of her life and sadly she too was taken from Angel all too soon. Yes, she had lost much in her life and was determined to have a more complete and happy life going forward.

There was much sumptuous food, mouth-watering deserts and great drinks during the wedding reception. It had been fun mingling and catching up with old friends. Angel had even caught the bouquet. Now the happy couple was headed for their honeymoon, leaving in a horse drawn carriage, to depart in the morning to an undisclosed location. If Angel could guess, she knew it would definitely be someplace warm with tropical beaches. If she knew anything about Viv, it was this: Viv did not like cold weather!

As much as Angel wanted to support Viv with her wedding, Angel was relieved that the search for a bridal gown and wedding were over. Now she could concentrate on the glaring nagging fact that had been plaguing her. Everyone had believed for years that she had been abducted by mistake. The note left in her room, *Jack, where is your most prized possession,* was a misdirection to steer everyone, including the police, down the wrong path. She now believed without a shadow of a doubt that she was indeed the intended victim in the kidnapping. Her proof was the fact that her room had been tossed despite the note that was left. From what she had learned about Raphael Medici, he was a diabolical villain and a master of subterfuge. Kidnapping Angel would devastate many for many different reasons.

Angel's quick call to Jamari, *Dad,* proved her suspicion. During their phone call Jamari revealed that in a shrewd move he had discovered the identity of his unknown investor, Raphael Medici. Jamari had gathered intel about Raphael from someone who owed

Jamari a favor. The intel revealed that Raphael Medici was behind a money laundering operation. Raphael had aligned himself with shady mobsters and Jamari intended to keep his business legitimate. He wanted no connection to this scoundrel. Through very strategic and stealthy maneuvering, Jamari was able to dislodge Raphael from his business. With Raphael losing a foothold in the export-import company, a perfect cover for his money laundering, and losing a good bit of money in the buyout, Medici planned revenge. He had been duped. What better way to get revenge on all in his delirium?

The irrational delusions of Raphael Medici struck at several individuals he held grievances with: Jack Montenero, Kyle Monroe - Paul's father - and Jamari and Damien Dupre. The late night meeting Jack arranged for he and Raphael many years, which Raphael bailed on, resulted in Serita Rodriguez, Raphael's then business partner, meeting Kyle Monroe. It did not matter that Raphael and Serita were not romantically involved. Raphael blamed Jack. Michelle may have been the target at first, but when Raphael learned Paul had feelings for Angelique, removing Angel was the way to hurt not only Jack, but Kyle through his son, Paul, and Jamari, her father. Raphael Medici gave no thought to Michelle's feelings.

Raphael cared little that he was Paul's godfather. To Raphael this was a slap in his face. To further hurt Jamari, Raphael intended to intensify Damien's angst through Angel, who was the reminder to Damien of all he lost after losing Michelle to Jamari. A wife and child. Angel was a carbon copy of Michelle and was the daughter that should have been Damien's. If Raphael could intensify the hard feelings between the two brothers, so much the better. In addition, Damien's silver bracelet, which Raphael held as collateral for a debt, was deliberately left at the scene of the crime to implicate Damien, and further hurt Jamari.

The puzzle pieces were finally falling into place. But the jury was still out on what Angel felt Paul was hiding. In the interim Angel began to spend more time with Edward. Before long a proposal of marriage came which Angel accepted. This decision pained Paul but he saw no way to convince Angel otherwise. She was moving on with her life with Edward for stability and companionship. True, Angel was too young to settle, but she convinced herself that she would be happy with Eddy even if she did not feel for him the way she did for Paul. Angel could trust Eddy and that was key.

A small wedding was in the planning similar to what Vivian and Jamal had planned. But Angel did not want a huge reception. Only her ten closest friends would be in attendance for the nuptials, which included her bridesmaid and Viv, the Matron of Honor. Afterward, the plan was to simply celebrate with a dinner for the couple in an upscale hotel with a string ensemble. They would spend their first night there as husband and wife and fly out to honeymoon in Hawaii the next day. Edward had wanted a huge event to announce to the world his love for Angel, but she was adamant. Her first marriage had been a lavish affair that soured soon after.

The nuptials were one month away and Angelique, with Vivian's help, was busy pulling everything together. At odd moments when she was alone Angel sensed a presence, a feeling that she was being watched still when she went out to run errands. Sweeping the area with a slow steady gaze, Angel crossed the street and entered Melanie's Bridal and Flowers to finalize the floral arrangements for the wedding venue - her home - and the banquet room at the hotel. Viv had found the musicians for the quiet dinner and reception after the nuptials, so all that was left was a final fitting for Angel's wedding gown. This dress would be a simple cream colored sleeveless sheath. Baby's breath would adorn her hair in lieu of a veil.

Edward's mother and father would dine with the couple along with Viv, Jamal, Jamari and his lady prior to the wedding. This would give Jamari a chance to finally meet his daughter's fiancé. Jamari would not miss this momentous occasion as he had before. Since Angel's trip to Miami father and daughter had grown close, calling each other two or three times a week. Jamari had missed so many years away from Angel, and had sadly only seen pictures of his granddaughter, Kimmie, who had passed away in a horrific accident.

Jamari now had a significant other, Gail Lafayette, who was originally from Louisiana, but who now resided in Miami. She would attend the wedding along-side Jamari. Angel had not met Gail, her dad's love interest, and possibly step-mother to be, but the two had spoken over the phone. Gail seemed to be a pleasant woman and Angel was glad her father had someone to center him.

~

In a quaint café located in an obscure part of town a large male figure sat hunched over a steaming cup of coffee. You could see from the way his short sleeve shirt fit his body that he was an athlete in superb form. And you could almost see the muscles rippling beneath his shirt with each slight movement. His legs, sprawled beneath the small table, were quite long so you could imagine how tall he would be standing. The only piece of jewelry he wore was an antique silver bracelet worn on this right wrist.

The lone figure was deep in thought, staring into space with an Amazon Fire tablet before him. He seemed to be mulling over a wedding announcement posted on the Washington Post website. The wedding announcement was for a noted local author, one Angelique Dupre Sterling, daughter of Jamari Dupre and the late Michelle Dupre and stepfather, Jack Montenero. The fiancé was Edward Morgan, editor of *NY Mag* and son of Dr. Helen and Atty. Gerald Morgan. A slight frown creased the forehead of this hulking pensive Adonis.

Across town Jamari and Gail were resting comfortably in their hotel room, having flown in a few days earlier for the pre wedding dinner for the parents and bridal party. Jamari was proud of his daughter and happy to be included in her life. He and Gail would be meeting Edward and his parents soon and Jamari was determined to have a private chat with the prospective groom to size him up. Despite what Angel had told him of Eddy, Jamari wanted to make sure he was suitable for his only daughter. He would be the one to *give away* Angel to her groom this time.

The wedding was now three days away. Everything was set. Only the final gown fitting remained on Angel's to do list, and that was set for 2:00 this afternoon. As she exited her condo to hop in her car a shadowy figure rounded the corner of the sidewalk at the end of her hedge, unseen by Angel. With the wedding on her mind Angel was preoccupied and paid little attention to her surroundings. After a short fifteen minute drive she pulled up to the parking lot to the boutique. As she exited her car Angel spied a tall figure looking her way in the doorway of a shop across the street. She merely glanced at the figure, then went on into the shop.

Beside the final fitting of the gown, Angel was picking up the dress she would be wearing to the dinner tonight for the parents and small wedding party. True to her word, Vivian had helped Angel select her bridal gown and the dress she would be wearing to the pre wedding dinner. Angel had chosen an elegant A-line scoop neck, knee-length tulle cocktail dress in dusty blue. Shimmering embroidery adorns the illusion scoop neck bodice that features graceful cap sleeves and a bold back cut-out. Matching scalloped lace trims the hem of the skirt. "Everything is coming together as planned," Angel sighed. However, if Angel had been more alert she would have paid more attention to the lone figure in the doorway. She might have even recognized the individual as none other than her benefactor, Damien Dupre, from years past.

~

There in the lobby of the Ritz-Carlton in Tysons Corner, Virginia stood a tall impeccably dressed Damien Dupre. Here stood a fine specimen of male virility. The eyes of every female to enter the building were riveted on this startlingly handsome man with seductive steel grey eyes and a well-groomed silken, auburn beard. Like his brother, Jamari, he too possessed a full head of chestnut brown hair with auburn streaks. But unlike Jamari, he stood 6'2'' tall with bulging muscles.

Patiently he stood, waiting for the small wedding part to arrive. The Dupre brothers had not seen each other in years, so it definitely came as a shock to Jamari to see the brother who was all but dead to him. Jamari left Gail and hurried to his brother.

"What are you doing here?" said Jamari. "Have you come to ruin things for me and my daughter?"

"Quite the opposite," replied Damien. "I've come to prevent a nightmare." Turning to the gawking onlookers, Damien singled out Edward and walked up to him. "Hello nephew," he boomed in his deep resonant voice.

Epilogue

Five Years Later

It was a balmy Spring morning. On the back porch of the two story structure sat Angel sipping on an iced tea while quietly rocking a sleeping infant boy in her arms. From the grass below came the playful sounds of three year old twins, Chris and Christine. From the path at the side of the house strode Edward carrying steaks and fresh sweet ears of corn for the grill. Right behind him came Monique, Jon and little sister, Stacie.

"You're right on time," called Paul. "The fire is just right."

"You know you can count on me, my man," replied Edward. "Who else is coming?"

"Vivian and Jamal and their brood should be here any minute with desserts; all the bases are covered," said Paul.

Today was only one of the many gatherings for the young friends. Damien indeed had prevented a catastrophe that fateful day at the Ritz-Carlton and ushered in new possibilities. With the revelation that Angel and Edward were actually close kin, Angel was greatly relieved she and Eddy had only shared a few kisses. Edward was the son of Damien's and Jamari's estranged older half-sister on their father's side. Helen, Edward's mother, was the daughter of that sister.

As fate would have it, the reunion of the century occurred that fateful day five years ago between the two brothers. Damien's main concern was protecting Angel, his niece, from a marriage that shouldn't happen and from any backlash Raphael Medici may have instigated from behind bars. Damien admitted he had been secretly watching out for Angelique once he came stateside during the past year. He feared Raphael might reach out from behind bars to strike their family again. He had stumbled on the wedding announcement by chance and knew he couldn't stay in the shadows any longer.

The most important thing to Angel had always been family, and now she had more family than she could have ever hoped for. Paul had come clean and finally admitted that Raphael had asked him to keep him apprised of Jack Montenero's whereabouts. Raphael had pretended to want to set up a business meeting between the two of them. Paul had carried that guilt for far too long. He had been a pawn in Raphael's scheme and Angel forgave him for that. How was he to know Raphael had malicious intent?! Paul hadn't set out to harm her family. He had just been earning money to return to college.

Oddly enough, Monique met Edward through Angelique and the two hit it off. Monique was truly a good and kind person. Angel could see why Paul had been drawn to her in his youth. But as she well knew, loving someone and being in love were two different things. Angel knew beyond a shadow of a doubt that Paul would always love Monique, the mother of his firstborn, but she knew he was in love with her. Paul was a devoted husband and father to their three children. It was perfect that Eddy had found Monique, fallen in love, married Monique and had a child with her. Eddy and Angel were family. Cousins. Now the four of them would always be tied together as one large family with Jon and little Stacie as an anchor between the two families.

Damien had become resolved with his demons of the past and had moved past the hurt of losing Michelle to Jamari. He had gained a niece he had come to care for on that deserted island long ago in the South Pacific. And Jamari was grateful to Damien for keeping Angel safe. Criminals often betray one another, and Jamari had found a loose thread in one thug. Once Jamari had plied this contact with enough drink he let slip that Raphael had *abducted some girl* in a revenge plot. More drink and cash provided the location, so Jamari was able to hire a rescue party for Angel.

Jamari also learned his brother, Damien, was an unwitting accomplice, so held no ill will toward him. He had recognized the bracelet found at the crime scene when described to him by Michelle. From discreet connections he was able to get the bracelet from police property and back to his brother through a mutual friend. Now that their differences were settled, the two brothers now worked together in the import-export business as partners.

You may not always like the family you're born into, but family always sticks together.

Study Questions

1. Describe the relationship between Angel and her mother, Michelle, and with her stepfather, Jack Montenero. Was it typical for a teenager? Why or why not? Describe the relationship between Angel and her father, Jamari. Was it manipulative, or did it arise from a genuine desire?

2. Does the long time friendship between Angel and Vivian seem genuine? Explain.

3. Do you believe Jamari betrayed Damien? Explain. Do you believe Paul experienced betrayal? If so, in what way?

4. Who else, if anyone, was betrayed in the novel? Explain your answer.

5. Explain Damien's initial behavior toward Angel during her captivity. What does this say about Damien? What does this say about Angel? Did Damien redeem himself? If so, how?

6. Trust is an issue for several characters. Which characters do you feel had trust issues? Did they overcome them? If so, how?

7. Paul and Monique are connected in a special way. Does Monique's behavior and reasoning seem real? Does she deserve forgiveness for her decisions, or do you feel Paul is responsible/at fault? Explain.

8. What are your thoughts on Vivian and Jamal's on again off again relationship? Did it seem real or contrived? Have you known anyone who has experienced this type of relationship? Should one keep fighting for the relationship or just move on? Explain.

9. Vivian and Angel seem to be polar opposites. Do you believe they balance each other? If so, tell how you see this happening. Give examples.

10. What was Damien's ritual with Angel during her captivity? What purpose did it serve?

11. Abandonment and loss are some of the themes in the novel. Where and with whom is this shown, and how do the affected characters handle this?

12. Raphael Medici blames others for his hurt. Is he justified or is he responsible for his own "injury"? Explain your answer.

13. What is your impression of Paul? Is he a static character throughout, or does his character grow? Explain.

14. Relationships between men and women at times are seen as difficult. Did the relationships between the characters seem realistic or contrived? Explain.

15. Is Angelique a weak or strong character? Give evidence to support your opinion.

16. Can you list any evidences of loyalty present in the novel? If so, describe.

17. What does the revelation of the half-sister reveal about family dynamics?

18. Were you surprised by the ending? Why or why not? Is this ending realistic/healthy? Explain.

About the Author

Rita Clark Johnson was born in Arlington, Virginia and now resides in Maryland. She worked in the health insurance industry twenty years in Washington, D. C., taught high school English in Philadelphia, Pennsylvania, was a Middle school Language Arts teacher in Lanham, Maryland and high school English teacher in Greenbelt, Suitland and Hyattsville, Maryland for almost as many years. She is a member of Alpha Kappa Alpha sorority through Cheyney University where she received her B.S. degree in English Education, and holds a Master of Education, Education Administration from Grand Canyon University. She is currently retired. This is her first novel.

www.ingramcontent.com/pod-product-compliance
Lightning Source LLC
Chambersburg PA
CBHW060329260626
47160CB00007B/2731